"I'm pregnant," Ruby blurted.

"You're what?" Matteo said, the words he most dreaded punching him in the stomach like two fists. "No," he started, shaking his head.

He was at the window—somehow. His hands were in his hair, on his face, in fists on the glass. He spun around.

"How can you be? Didn't we... Weren't you..."

He paced again—to the bathroom. He opened the door and turned on the tap, let cold water gather into his hands and splashed it on his face. He stared at himself in the mirror.

A father? That wasn't the face of a father!

He wasn't cut out for that. He wasn't even cutting his own path in life—he hadn't filled his father's shoes in business—never mind having a kid of his own. He could never be a father, not now, like this.

He walked back out. She was still there, standing exactly as he'd left her.

Dear God, what had he done?

Silent, soulful sobs began to rack her body. He thought of his mother's face, his father's smile, the mess he'd made of his life...

And this woman, this beautiful creature standing before him, now sharing a life between them.

Unable to sit still without reading, **Bella Frances** first found romantic fiction at the age of twelve, in between deadly dull knitting patterns and recipes in the pages of her grandmother's magazines. An obsession was born! But it wasn't until one long, hot summer, after completing her first degree in English literature, that she fell upon the legends that are Harlequin books. She has occasionally lifted her head out of them since to do a range of jobs, including barmaid, financial adviser and teacher, as well as to practice (but never perfect) the art of motherhood to two (almost grown-up) cherubs.

Bella lives a very energetic life in the UK but tries desperately to travel for pleasure at least once a month—strictly in the interests of research!

Catch up with her on her website at bellafrances.co.uk.

Books by Bella Frances

Harlequin Presents

The Playboy of Argentina
The Scandal Behind the Wedding
The Consequence She Cannot Deny

Claimed by a Billionaire

The Argentinian's Virgin Conquest
The Italian's Vengeful Seduction

Bella Frances

THE TYCOON'S
SHOCK HEIR

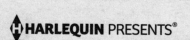
HARLEQUIN PRESENTS®

Recycling programs
for this product may
not exist in your area.

ISBN-13: 978-1-335-47795-8

The Tycoon's Shock Heir

First North American publication 2018

Copyright © 2018 by Bella Frances

Printed in U.S.A.

THE TYCOON'S SHOCK HEIR

To my son, Harry

With all my love

CHAPTER ONE

FRIDAY AFTERNOON. BEST TIME in the world. Working week wrapped up and the party just about to start. And, with the news he'd just heard, Matteo Rossini knew it was going to be some party.

He stepped out of the car, loosened his tie and took the steps into his jet for the last task of the day—the short flight from Rome to London and a call to the Executive Director, Signora Rossini herself. Mamma to him.

He walked through the cabin and sat at his desk, ready to sink his Friday beer. It wasn't there.

He slung his bag on the empty chair and looked around. Neither was his assistant David. Strange. They had this routine down—the beer, the call, some water, some press-ups, shower and change, the car ready in London, sometimes a woman, sometimes not. Tonight was definitely a 'sometimes not' night. Tonight was boxing, a little gambling and all-male bonding—as soon as he delivered the news.

He sat down and keyed in the number. Drummed

his fingers. Looked around again for David. Where *was* he?

At the sound of a beer being opened he turned, just as the call connected. He noticed the legs first, then the red dress. Definitely not David. He frowned and swivelled away from the sight as the bottle was placed beside him. Someone had some explaining to do.

'Hey, it's me.'

'Matteo! Good. I was just going to call you.'

'Well, here I am. With some news.'

'OK? You first, then.'

His heart raced. This was it.

'Arturo is finally selling. And we've got first refusal.' He touched the beer bottle, waited to hear his mother's response.

'Seriously? After all this time? That's incredible news.'

Matteo allowed his fingers to close round the neck of the bottle. Indeed it was.

'How did you find out?'

'It wasn't hard. I heard a rumour and did a little digging. Word is he's had enough. He wants out and we're the only ones in the running...'

He let the sentence dangle in the air. Even over the thousand miles that separated them he could imagine the mixture of heartache and hunger on his mother's face.

'You're absolutely sure about that?'

He paused. There was no point in pretending.

'We're the only ones properly in the running. I heard Claudio's going to throw his hat in the ring. But he's poison. His reputation has travelled to Switzerland, I guarantee it. He hasn't got a chance.'

'Matty, I don't want you to get involved.'

Her tone sank further than the ground beneath the plane.

'Mamma. You know this is the one that matters. Claudio walked away with half our clients and now I'm going to get them back. If we merge with Arturo we'll be unstoppable. I can do this. I promise you.'

'I don't want you to promise anything, Matty. I don't want you losing your mind the way your father did. It's not worth it. Nothing's worth it.'

He sighed and released his hand from the bottle. He had known she'd feel like this and he couldn't blame her, but they'd never get another chance.

'I can't let it pass—you know that,' he said quietly. 'Come on, Mamma. For Dad. We can't let Claudio get one over on us again.'

He waited for her to speak, but the plane climbed through silence. He could imagine the worry knitting her fine brows, twin tracks of loss and anguish. The look that had haunted her for years.

But she was Coral Rossini. And he was her son…

'You're right. We can't let that happen,' she said finally. 'We can't sit back and let him walk all over us again.'

'Exactly,' he said, letting out a breath.

'But you have to promise me that if he tries to do

anything you'll walk away. Matteo. Promise me. I can't lose a husband *and* a son.'

The image of his father lying across the dashboard of his car flashed through his mind and he clenched his jaw so hard he could almost taste metal. Metal that he would use to grind Claudio's bones to dust. One day.

'You have nothing to fear, Mamma.'

'I have everything to fear. I couldn't bear anything to happen to you.'

The break in her voice killed him. She had more strength and resilience than anyone else alive. The fact that they could even say the name 'Claudio' in a conversation now was testament to how far they'd come. That man had been closer than family, his father's best friend, his trusted lawyer then partner, and he'd sold them out—right under their noses. No one had been able to believe he'd set it all up and got away with it. And the rest. The unspeakable dark shadow he'd cast over their lives.

All they could do was put one foot in front of the other and try to salvage Banca Casa di Rossini— the two-hundred-year-old private bank of the Italian super-rich.

'Nothing's going to happen other than us taking the bank back to where it should be. Even if we don't get all of Arturo's clients we'll outrank Claudio. And that's all that matters, isn't it?'

The plane hit a patch of turbulence and Matty looked out at the thick grey cloud wrapping itself over the Italian countryside, Not even a thunderstorm was going to dim his spirits. Not with this rainbow on the horizon. Handing their crock of gold back to his mother had been his dream for years.

'What about the name? We might need to change the bank's name. Have you thought of that?'

'I'm ahead of you. If it comes to it, I'll do it. BAR. Banca Arturo Rossini. How does that sound?'

'Oh, Matty…'

He heard the wistful note in her voice. He felt it too. The bank went back generations, was respected the world over. But it was live or die. There was no third way.

'It's not what I want, but if it's the only way… We really do have a chance with this, don't we?'

Matty looked up as the woman in red walked past him down the aisle, the satin of her dress catching the light with every slow, steady step. His eyes zoned in on her legs again. They were quite something. And the way the skirt swished gently above her elegant calves with every step she took triggered a strong response. An unwelcome response.

'Matty?'

'We've got a really great chance,' he said, refocusing. 'There's no other private bank that reeks of old money and old values like ours. Claudio has turned his bank into just another sales-driven call centre. There's nothing sure and solid and *honest* about it. We're unique. Second only to Arturo in terms of stature.'

'I know. We just have to hope that stature and honesty are what he's looking for.'

'It's going to be all about the chemistry. And the fact that we've still not floated on the stock exchange. That's why we're ahead of Claudio—no matter what kind of offer he makes Arturo. I'm sure of it. In fact, I'm so sure I'm going to bet you that I land an invitation to Arturo's villa when we're at the Cordon D'Or Regatta. It's going to be a slow burn, but that's where I intend to start.'

He turned at the sound of water being poured. A squat crystal glass was placed down. He saw long, elegant fingers. Long, slim arms bare in the strapless red dress. And beaming down at him the dimpled smile of an angel.

'Thanks.' He frowned, automatically turning his head to watch her walk away. Mistake. His eyes narrowed on the smooth white skin above the red bodice of her dress, the delicate bones and long, swanlike neck. She was absolutely beautiful.

He was far too busy to allow himself any distractions. What the hell was David playing at?

'That'll be a start. But it'll take more than a little corporate hospitality at the Cordon D'Or to win him over. He's the last of the old guard. You'd better make sure your social media profile is squeaky clean. If there's a hint of any more scandal he'll pull up his drawbridge before you get within a mile of it.'

'There won't be any more. You can rely on that.'

He bitterly regretted there being any at all. And

the timing was a disaster. He drummed his fingers on the window, traced the water droplets as they shook their way across the glass. His media presence had never been an issue before. Not until his most recent ex, Lady Faye, had started to feed the story of their break-up to the press. Now he was the 'City Love Rat', destroying the life of any woman who got close, stringing her along with promises of marriage and then dumping her disgracefully.

The truth was nothing like that. He never promised anything beyond the first date—as every one of his ex-girlfriends could testify.

Over the years he had carefully developed the symptoms of full-blown commitment phobia—the best possible illness for any confirmed bachelor to suffer from. Married to the job. Workaholic. Unashamedly, indubitably *yes*. He didn't commit to anything he couldn't see through to the end and he would never, ever commit to a woman the way he had once committed to his first love, Sophie.

He had lost his dad, lost his path in life and then lost her. There would be no more loss. He'd never be that vulnerable again.

'I wish you'd let David handle it. We could have done some damage limitation at least.'

'It's not my style. I refuse to play the games those trashy media sharks want me to play. And I won't get involved in any tit-for-tat about something that is nobody's business. Faye was ill. That's the only explanation. She believed something that wasn't real and then when it didn't fall into place the way she imagined she took it to the press the way she did with everything else. If she wasn't minor royalty no one would have cared, and me weighing in with "my story" would have been the last thing to make it better. That would have just prolonged the whole sorry mess.'

'I know that. But because you refused to even make a statement people think you're some sort of pariah. I hate anybody to think badly of you when I know what you're really like. It upset me reading that stuff.'

'So do as I do and don't read it.'

He heard her sigh and it cut him. It was easy for him to brush it off. What did *he* care what a bunch of people who didn't know him thought? It was ridiculous, worrying about stuff like that. But his mother was different. She cared. Deeply. About him and the bank. And everyone else too. She cared too much.

'I'm sorry, Mamma. But I can't turn the clock back. It'll all blow over and then it'll be some other poor sod's turn to be vilified.'

The woman in red was reaching up to put linens in the cupboard. Her arms were as slender and pale as long-stemmed lilies, her moves graceful and elegant. Her hair hung in a dark ponytail down her back, shiny and thick and long. She turned to glance at him, her dark eyes coy and unsure. He knew that look. He knew where it could go...

'Hang on.' He walked to the bedroom at the other

end of the cabin and closed the door. 'Have you heard from David? He's not here and some woman is in his place. It's totally out of character for him just to send in agency staff like this...'

'Ah, I think you must be talking about Ruby. What do you think? Isn't she lovely?'

His mother had that excited tone in her voice that made him instantly aware...

'That's not in dispute,' he said. 'But I was hoping David would be looking after things for me until I said otherwise. What's going on?'

'Don't get upset, Matty. I'm up to my eyes and I needed David to finish off the branding work with the new advertising agency. No one knows our business better than him.'

'You've pulled rank and left me with a newbie?'

'I met Ruby,' she said, ignoring him, 'and I was very impressed. She's a fast learner—I think you two will get along fine. And you'll have David back on Monday.'

His mother was still holding something back. He was sure of it.

'You know she's dressed in a cocktail dress? A very nice cocktail dress, but it's not exactly work wear. Is there something else you've forgotten to tell me?'

Like last month, when she'd only remembered to tell him he had to make an after-dinner speech at the International Women in Finance dinner an hour before the canapés were served. Or the time when he'd had to present a prize at a kindergarten they sponsored on the way home from the casino. It was getting to be a bit of a habit, her asking him these last-minute 'favours' now that she was neck-deep in charity work.

'Ah. Now you mention it…'

Here it came.

'I'm afraid I'm still in Senegal, and there is one *tiny* engagement that needs to be covered tonight. You're in London anyway—so it's right on your doorstop. And who knows? Maybe you'll net some good press coverage from it too! Wouldn't that be lovely? Matty? Are you still there?'

Matty's fingers slid down the veneer of the door as one by the one all his party plans burst like bubbles in champagne.

'It's for charity, darling. The underprivileged.'

Of course it was. It was what she did. While he took care of the nuts and bolts of the business she got on with all the charity and philanthropy. She was amazing at getting the rich and famous to part with cash and favours for the various charities the bank sponsored. It worked perfectly well—if only she would remember to tell him when she needed him.

'OK. You've guilt-tripped me. I'm in.' He sighed. 'What's involved?'

'It's an arts benefit premiere at the King's.'

'As long as it's not dance. You know I can't stand men in tights.'

'Did you say dance? Yes, it's my favourite company—the British Ballet. Don't groan, darling. All you have to do is a quick photo-call on the red carpet and shake some hands afterwards. Everything is arranged. I know you like to be prepared, so I've asked Ruby to look after things. She has your itinerary, and there's nothing she doesn't know about dance. She's one of the British Ballet's soloists, but she's recovering from injury at the moment—a dreadful year she's had, poor thing.'

He opened the door into the cabin and right on cue the gorgeous Ruby appeared. So she wasn't agency staff—she was a dancer. Well, that checked out. Her posture was perfect…her body was perfect. But why on earth was she serving him iced water at twenty thousand feet?

Suddenly it all became clear.

He went back into the bedroom and closed over the door.

'This is a roundabout way of saying that you met someone with another hard luck story and took her under your wing.'

'I know what you're thinking and I'm not going to lie. Ruby's had a tough time, but she's not a victim. This isn't all a one-way street, so you can relax.'

'Well, what is it, then?'

His mother was always feeling sorry for some waif or stray, and they didn't all have the best of intentions. He'd had years rooting out the swindlers and the chancers from the genuinely broken people who seemed to flock towards her. For all she was a shrewd businesswoman, she was also immensely gullible when it came to anyone with a hard luck story.

'Matty, there is nothing for you to worry about! Ruby is not going to trick me out of my millions. She's completely dedicated to the British Ballet, but she's off with an injury so this is her way of keeping involved. But if you'd rather have one of the men in tights I'm sure that can be arranged...?'

He shook his head in disbelief. Once again she'd twisted him around her little finger. How could he resist anything his mother said? After all she'd done for him, holding it together all these years. They were tight—a unit. They had been since his father's death and always would be. It was that simple.

And if ever he had a moment when he doubted anything he heard his father's voice—his conscience, whatever—whispering in his ear. There was no way his mother's wishes would go unheeded. Ever.

'OK. As long as she doesn't get the wrong idea.'

'That part's entirely up to you, Matteo.'

He caught the slight note of censure in her voice—and the double meaning. She knew his vices as much as he did himself. The fact that he didn't want a long-term relationship didn't mean that he wanted to spend his evenings alone.

'OK, Mamma. I didn't mean with me, but we'll let that pass.'

'I'm sorry, darling, I don't mean to have a dig. But it upsets me that women are so disposable to you.

I know you could have a happy life if only you'd let yourself settle down with someone. At the end of the day I'm your mother, and I only want what's best for you.'

'What's best for me is what's best for the bank. That's all I'm interested in. Not settling down with a woman. I'm not saying that I'll always feel this way, but for now, until I've got past this hurdle, the bank is all there is.'

The words were out. As plain as numbers on a balance sheet. Irrevocable. No room for misinterpretation. Profit. Loss. Black. White. No shades of grey, no emotion colouring things. Just following the dream. His father's dream. And now it was his. Like it or not.

CHAPTER TWO

FLIGHT AT SIX, land at seven-thirty, less an hour for time difference. Half-hour to get to the theatre. It would be a miracle if she pulled it off without a hitch.

Ruby stood in the middle of the cabin and stared— left to the cockpit and right, all the way to the firmly closed bedroom door, where Matteo Rossini, company sponsor, heart-throb and all-round Love Rat was still taking calls while the minutes ticked past.

She shook her head and stared down at her arms, where blotches and hives were beginning their stress march across her skin—a sure sign that she was out of her comfort zone.

It was bad enough that she'd been on the bench for months, waiting for this ligament damage to heal, but now she was hurtling towards London, and the world premiere of *Two Loves*, with the job of convincing their sponsor that the British Ballet was worth every penny of the money his private bank channelled their way.

So much responsibility—and she was the last person they should have trusted to do this.

If it had been Coral Rossini herself it would have been fine. She was the Grande Dame of Dance. She'd been a massive support to the company for years. She was loved and gave love in return, supporting them at every premiere. But not this time. This time her second-in-command was stepping in.

And when the director had passed Ruby that note, with a *Who's the lucky girl?* look on his face, it had been all she could do to stop herself from groaning aloud, *Hopefully not me...*

She'd read Coral Rossini's note.

So lovely to meet you again yesterday!

I've suddenly realised you would be the ideal person to look after my son Matteo at the benefit on Friday. He's not the biggest fan of dance but I'm sure you'll work your magic.

I have taken the liberty of sending some things for you. And some things for Matteo to wear too.

Don't worry if he puts up a fight—he's a pussycat really!

Ciao!

Coral x

She'd stared at the note, her heart tumbling into her stomach, and then opened the bags and boxes of clothes, all beautifully wrapped and folded in tissue.

There had been the red dress—a froth of satin and petticoats—a wrap with a beautiful Chinese poppy print, beige court shoes and a little matching clutch. Then she'd found a red tie and pocket square for Matteo to wear, and tucked into an envelope was a cheque for a thousand pounds.

A thousand pounds! That had made it even more impossible to say no. No one could afford to turn her nose up at that kind of money. But for *this*? She just wasn't cut out for schmoozing with the people who hung around the fringes of the dance world. She couldn't care less who was famous or rich or both.

The director had been quite up-front about it.

'I can trust you to do it. Some of the other girls might get a bit carried away, but you've got your head screwed on. You'll not let us down. Or yourself...'

He was right about that. She'd been with the British Ballet longer than anyone else—it had been home and school and friends and family to her for years. She'd come up through the ranks from eleven years old and she had no ambition to go anywhere else or do anything else. She was safe there. It was all she knew. And all she wanted to know.

Others came, made friends, found lovers, moved on. They had lives outside of the studio and the theatre. They went to parties and spoke about their families. They knew not to ask her about hers. She knew they were curious, but they accepted her silence. Who'd want to talk about that, after all? The gap year father who just kept on travelling, and the teenage mother who hadn't been able to accept the curfew demanded by a newborn baby.

Thank God for dance. That was her silent prayer. Without dance she would still be the millstone around her mother's neck or the fatherless obsessive—scouring the internet, searching for his face in the crowd, dreaming about reconciliations that would never happen...

'Hi. I'm Matteo. Good to meet you.'

She startled at the sound of his voice and dropped the bag of peanuts she'd been about to open.

Deep breath, big smile, and turn.

'Ruby. Hello.' She smiled as she neatly grabbed the bag and extended her hand.

She had to admit he was even more of a heart-throb up close—and so *tall*. His tie hung loosely, like a rope on the wall of his wide chest. She gazed up past thick broad shoulders to a blunt jaw and a full-lipped mouth. His nose was broad and long, broken at the bridge, and his eyes, when she reached them, were sharp brown berries, tucked deep into a frown.

He shook her hand. Warmly...firmly. Then dropped his hand away. She found herself staring at the half-smile on his lips, noticing how wide and full they were, and thinking that with his longer-than-collar-length hair he looked more like a romantic poet trapped in a boxer's body than a boring banker.

'Everything OK?'

Bang, bang, bang. Words were fired out like bullets at a target, and his eyes were taking in everything. *Every. Thing.* They darted all over her face and swept up the rest of her—and maybe it was the close confines of the plane, or the fact that he had such a *presence*, or the fact that she was not used to standing in heels serving drinks to a total stranger at twenty thousand feet, but her footing faltered and she had to reach out to hold the back of a seat for balance.

'Yes. I—I was just going to pour you another drink and find some snacks and...'

'No problem. I'm fine for drinks and snacks. But apparently I'm heading to the ballet now, which is quite a turn of events.'

'Yes,' she said, regaining perfect balance and poise. 'To see *Two Loves*. The premiere. We're so excited. It's an amazing production.'

And it was. And she'd have given anything to be in it. But because of this hideous injury she wasn't even in the corps. Instead she'd had to pack her day with teaching junior classes and attending physio. And serving Love Rats...

'And you're the face of the British Ballet. That's good. That's really good,' he said, scanning her again and nodding as if in fact it was really bad. 'Done your homework, I take it? I'll need to know the names and the bios of the people we're going to see.'

He moved around the cabin now and she stood there, not quite sure if she was supposed to follow him, reassure him, or disappear off the face of the earth.

She watched him turn on a screen that flashed

stock exchange numbers. He glanced at it, then changed it quickly to sports. He folded his arms and stared at the screen as a commentator's voice rose to a crescendo over the roar of a crowd. She looked to see what it was—men charging into one another, with mud-splattered thighs as big as tree trunks, ears and noses like Picasso paintings, all grabbing for an oval shaped ball as if it was the Holy Grail. Rugby. *Yuck.* How could anyone get excited about that?

'Come on!' he grunted at the players on the screen as he moved towards it.

Obviously Matteo Rossini did. She waited…and watched, but it was as if she had become a part of the furniture, as incidental as the beige leather chairs. He might have the looks, but he had none of his mother's charm.

Suddenly he turned, caught her gawping, and frowned. He pressed the remote control 'off' and tossed it down on the chair.

'I have plans for later, so I'd like this to be all wrapped up by ten. Shall we make a start?'

He nodded, indicating the little lounge area where four leather armchairs were grouped around a coffee table. He lowered himself down, comfortable, confident and totally composed, while she perched carefully, straight-backed, knees locked, smile fixed.

'OK. Basics first. You're a dancer with this ballet company, but you've "volunteered" to take on this PR role just for tonight.'

'Something like that,' she said, ignoring the air quotes he made with his hands.

'So what's Ruby's story? Why you?' he said, narrowing his eyes and steepling his fingers.

'You want to know about me? There's not much to tell. I've been with the BB since I was eleven,' she said, realising that she was now being interviewed for a job she didn't even want. 'I'm not dancing tonight, so I think I was the obvious choice.'

'The BB is the British Ballet?'

She smiled at his stupid question.

'Yes. The company's fifty years old. I've been in the school, the corps, then a soloist and hopefully one day a principal. So I know everything there is to know.'

'What about the other side of things? There will be political points being scored here tonight. You know everything there is to know about that too, I take it?'

As she stared at him she suddenly remembered the notes. Had she brought them? Pages and pages of silly handwritten notes about all the other stuff she was meant to tell him. She'd been writing them out in the kitchen, she'd numbered them, she'd stacked them... And then what had she done with them?

'You're prepared, right? One thing you should know about me is I'm not a big fan of winging it.'

Neither am I, she wanted to answer back. Which was why she had spent so long making notes about things she didn't find remotely interesting. But being rude to the sponsor was not an option—not with all that revenue riding on it. Her own scholarship had been funded through the generosity of patrons like Coral Rossini, the Company Director had been quick to remind her.

'I'm sure you won't be disappointed. Mrs Rossini was confident I was right for the job.'

'Yes. I'm sure she was,' he said, in a tone that buzzed in her subconscious like an annoying fly.

But where *were* the notes? In her bag? Or could she have stuffed them in her pockets? Left them on the Tube?

He tipped his head back, scrutinised her with a raised brow, looking down the length of his annoyingly handsome nose, and she wondered if he could read her mind.

'How long have you known my mother, incidentally? She seems to have taken quite a shine to you.'

'She has?'

She'd definitely had the notes just before she got in the car...

'Yes. And you wouldn't be the first person to want to be friends with my incredibly kind, incredibly generous mother.'

What was he talking about? Did he think that she wanted to be his mother's friend? Did he think she actually *wanted* to be here, doing this?

'I'm not here to make friends with anyone. I'm here because I was told to be.'

And then she stopped, suddenly aware of the dark

look that had begun to spread across his face. She'd gone too far.

'You were *told* to be?' he asked as his brows rose quizzically above those sharp sherry-coloured eyes.

'Someone had to do it.'

He sat back now, framed in the cream leather seat, elbows resting on the arms of the chair and fingers steepled in front of his chest. They were shaded with fine dark hair, and above the pinstriped cuff of his shirt the metallic gleam of a luxury watch twinkled and shone.

She kept her eyes there, concentrating on the strong bones of his wrists, refusing to look into his face as the jet powered on through the sky.

'And you drew the short straw?' he said, lifting his water.

She caught sight of the solid chunks of burnished silver cufflinks. She'd never even known anyone who wore cufflinks before, barely knew anyone who bothered to wear a shirt and tie, and she wondered for a moment how he got them off at night.

'You'd rather be anywhere other than here?'

His voice curled out softly, quietly, just above the thrum of the engines, and with the unmistakable tone of mockery. Was he teasing her? She flashed a glance up. He was. The tiniest of smiles lurked at the corner of his mouth. Did that mean he *didn't* think she was trying to stick her claws into his mother?

Maybe.

She shifted in the chair, used her core muscles to

keep from slipping further down into the bucket seat. He sat completely still, and with all that *body* sitting across from her it was impossible to concentrate.

'I'd rather be performing,' she said. 'Nothing matters more to me than that.'

'That I understand,' he said quietly. His face fell for a moment as some other world held him captive. He opened and flexed his hand, turned it around and she saw knuckles distended, broken. 'I understand that very well.'

She looked down at her own hands, bunched up on her lap in the scarlet satin, and waited for him to speak. He didn't. He crossed his leg and her gaze travelled there. And all the way along it. All the way along hard, strong muscle. She knew firm muscle when she saw it, and he was even better built than a dancer—bulkier, stronger, undeniably masculine. She could make out powerful thighs under all that navy silk gabardine, and the full force of the shoulders stretched out under his shirt. He could lift her above his head, and spin her around, lay her down and then…

He laid his hands on the armrests and she glanced up, startled out of her daydream.

'Sorry. I— Let's get back on track.' She cleared her throat. OK, time to remember her notes. 'The performance tonight. You want me to give you the details now?'

'Please do.' He nodded.

She frowned. She could repeat every dance

step, but that wasn't what he needed to know. Details. Names. Dates. All in the notes, in a pile, on her kitchen table—which was at least five hundred miles away.

'*Two Loves* is based on a poem.'

'A poem…? Anything more specific than that?'

Yes, there were specifics. Loads of specifics. She'd written them down, memorised them, but fishing them out of her brain now was a different thing. As if she needed any more reminding that the one single thing she could do in life was dance. She was completely hopeless at almost everything else.

'It's…really old,' she said, grasping for any single fact.

His eyebrow was still raised. 'How old? Last month? Last year? Last century?'

'Ancient old,' she said, an image of the poet that the choreographer had shown them coming to mind. 'Like two thousand years. And Persian,' she said happily. 'It's all coming back. He's a Persian poet called Rumi, famous for his love poems.'

'Ah yes. Rumi. *"Lovers don't finally meet somewhere. They're in each other all along…"* And all that rubbish.'

'Yes, well. Some of that—"rubbish"—has made this ballet tonight,' she said, pleased that she'd remembered something, even if he sounded less than impressed.

'OK. Though, since its unlikely I'm going to be shaking hands with the poet Rumi tonight, do you have any facts about anyone alive? There's normally a whole list of people I need to thank.'

'Yes,' she said, staring into his unimpressed face. 'That's all in my notes.'

'Right,' he said, standing up and staring at his watch. 'We land in thirty minutes. You get your notes and I'll grab a shower and get into my tux.' He looked at her and nodded. 'I think we're both agreed that the sooner we get this over with the better.'

CHAPTER THREE

Matteo Rossini was sacking off boxing and the casino to go to the ballet? Was he for real?

He could hear the boys howling down the phone as they all raised their glasses in a fake toast. At least someone found it funny, he thought as he hauled his third-best tux out of the wardrobe and laid it out on the bed.

He'd been looking forward to this night for ages. A chance to really blow off steam after the disastrous media circus he'd lived through with Faye. And learning of the juicy prospect of tucking Arturo Finance into the back pocket of the bank was going to be the icing on the cake.

He felt he was almost on the home straight already.

But all that would have to wait while he went to the ballet.

He dragged the towel across his damp shoulders and chuckled, realising he wasn't nearly as down about it as he'd been half an hour ago. And it didn't have anything to do with a new desire to watch people flounce about the stage. All the charm of the evening was wrapped up in one beautiful little package called Ruby.

She might well have designs on his mother, but he wasn't getting that feeling from her—he wasn't picking up that sycophantic thing that most people had about them when they met him for the first time.

She was refreshing, and he was in the mood to be refreshed, and since there was no choice in the matter for the next couple of hours he might as well enjoy what he could.

He stepped into his trousers just as there was a knock on the door. He listened. It came again. Two tiny little raps—one-two. Quiet, but determined. Business not pleasure, he thought, registering with interest a slight sense of disappointment.

He fastened his flies and lifted his shirt, then opened the door and there she was. All eyes, lips and lily-white slender limbs.

'Hello, there,' he said, stretching his arms inside his shirt. 'Everything OK?'

By the look on her face everything was *not* OK. Her eyes had widened to coal-black circles and her mouth was in a shocked red 'O' as she gawped at his chest. He stifled a smile as he turned to spare her blushes and started to button his shirt.

'I'm so sorry to bother you,' she said, tucking her eyes down, 'but I was meant to give you this to wear.' She held out a little parcel, kept her head turned away. 'From your mum.'

He continued to fasten his buttons and stared at the little parcel.

'Want to open it for me?' he said, now walking to the table for his cufflinks.

Her eyes flicked up, then down, but not before she took a good long look. He couldn't help but smile broadly. *Game on.*

She pulled open the package and held out a red bow tie and pocket square.

'Is everything OK?'

'What?' she said. 'Yes, of course everything is OK. I was just wondering why you bother with those things.'

He paused, his collar up, considering her carefully. That was not what he'd expected to hear.

'Pardon?'

'Cufflinks. What are they even for? Why not just use buttons? I don't get it.'

'Has anyone ever told you you're quite forward?' he said, clicking the cufflinks together.

'I say what's on my mind. I'm not trying to cause offence, but I've never seen anyone use them.'

He finished and tugged at his cuffs, checking that his sleeves were perfectly straight, watching her watching him carefully. He was warming to her more by the minute.

'They make my cuffs sit nicely. I like the look. A beautiful shirt deserves beautiful cuffs. And, since you're looking unconvinced by that answer, I'll also add that these were a gift from an ex-girlfriend. After we split up.'

He turned them in the light and smiled.

'I'm not all Mr Bad Guy, despite what you might have read in the press.'

'Oh,' she said. 'Right…' with a tone that was flat and disbelieving.

He raised an eyebrow and tied the bowtie in place.

Well, what did he expect? he thought, turning away to get his jacket while his mind ran to the stupid pictures his friends had texted him and those quotes about being emotionally stunted.

He hadn't bothered to read them properly. Anyone who knew him well knew the truth. And anyone who knew him well knew that all his stunted emotions sat with Sophie. The only thing he was sure of in his life was that there would never be another Sophie…

They had been the Golden Couple all through university—she with her long blonde hair and he a rising star of the rugby scene. He'd never been happier. The whole world had been spread out before him. His degree in sports science, his imminent career as a rugby player, playing for his country… Would it be Italy or England? When would he ask Sophie to marry him? Where would they live?

Those were the kinds of decisions he'd faced. Until the night he'd got the news that his father had died. Like a great oak being ripped up from the roots, his strength, his confidence had been sapped. He'd felt the world crumble under his feet, felt himself spinning in space. He'd thought his father sure and solid and strong. He'd had all the answers. He'd been wise and clever and honourable and he'd loved his mother—and Claudio had been his best friend.

They had been almost inseparable—closer than brothers. The only thing that had ever came between his parents had been Claudio's suffocating presence in their lives—until something had happened and everything had changed.

Matteo had once suspected that Claudio had made a move on his mother and his father had found out. It had to be something like that for the schism between them to have been so deep. How wrong he had been.

His father's fight to save the family bank had been epic. He had worked tirelessly for weeks, but so much of it had gone. People with lots of money wanted lots more. Loyalty was too expensive. Especially when Claudio had offered a fast dividend and people had been too greedy to care how it was made.

But it had been his father's death more than the losses to the company that had devastated Matteo's life. His mother had been inconsolable—the thought of her anguish still made him wince with pain. He had gone to her side, nursed her and taken charge as he knew his father would have wanted. A stream of people from the banking world had arrived—all firm handshakes, sober suits and quiet conversations.

All of that he had lived through, knowing that it

couldn't get any worse. Knowing that Sophie was there for him.

And the knowledge of her warm, loving body had driven him one night to take a flight north to university, then a two-hour taxi ride from the airport to the cold, stormy coast of St Andrew's, where he'd known she would be just about to wake up. Maybe he'd slip into bed beside her, feel the love in her arms and bury himself and his pain...

How many times must he relive those moments? The crunch of the gravel, the lightening shadows of the morning and the frosted cloud of his breath. The cold, metallic slide of his key in the lock, lamps still burning in the hallway, the TV on, glasses on the table.

Like an automaton he had turned to the sound of the shower.

And then had come the sight he wished he could burn from his eyes.

His beautiful Sophie, naked and wet, her legs wrapped around another man. And the other man had been the national rugby coach, come all the way to Scotland to ask him to play for his country.

Was he emotionally stunted? All day long. And for the rest of his life.

'Most people don't believe what they read. I never do, if it's any consolation.'

His eyes tracked round, following the voice that had split through the sick daydream. Angel-faced Ruby, with those huge brown eyes and wide red lips was looking up at him with something that might be described as concern. How sweet. But if it was concern, it was wasted.

'Please don't worry about me,' he said, fastening the last button on his jacket. 'I'm a big boy. I can take what they dish up and swallow it whole.'

He winked. He smiled. He put one hand on her shoulder. Her delicate, silken-skinned shoulder. He stepped a little closer and watched as her eyes did that widening thing that women always did—usually just before he leaned in for his first kiss...

And wouldn't a kiss be the perfect way to start his evening with Ruby? Those gorgeous lips, that ivory skin, her lustrous hair... Hadn't he been tempted from the moment he'd seen her? Hadn't she shown that she was tempted too?

This could turn into the perfect night after all.

Oh, yes, he thought, and the stirring and hardening in his groin were now very obviously happening. There was only one thing left to do.

'But it must hurt your mother—reading that,' she said, turning her head.

He paused in mid-air, correcting himself and exiting the move swiftly. He'd been rebuffed. Well, well, well...

'What my mother feels is no concern of yours or anyone else's,' he heard himself say. 'I wish people would leave well alone.'

Colour rose like a scarlet tide over her cheeks and he instantly regretted his sharp tone.

Damn, that had been too harsh. Ruby didn't seem like the gossipy type. And she was only being kind. And, worst of all, she was right. He knew his mother had been hurt by the press, and he knew he had no one to blame for that but himself.

But why couldn't people worry about their own lives instead of raking all over his?

He reached out a hand—an involuntary gesture—but she muttered an apology under her breath and was already making her way back through the cabin. He watched her walk carefully, the red satin billowing out above her calves, swishing gently with each step, until he was almost hypnotised by the sight.

And then the plane bumped and dropped. And she stumbled. She reached out to grab at the nearest chair and held on to it for two long seconds. He could tell she was holding herself in pain. She didn't utter a sound.

He rushed to her.

'Are you OK?'

'Perfectly, thanks,' she said, keeping her eyes ahead and fixing that smile in place as she started to walk again.

'I saw you stumble there. Is it your injury? I know that's why you're not dancing at the moment. Is everything OK?'

She raised her eyebrows and flicked him an *as if you care* glance. He deserved that.

'I'm fine, thanks. I'm going to sit down now, if that's OK.'

'Ruby—hold up.'

She sat carefully in the seat, straightening her spine, and her bright smile popped back into place. He recognised that—smiling through pain. Everybody had a mask.

He sat in the seat opposite her. She tucked her knees to the left and pressed them together, sitting even straighter—a clearer Keep Back message he'd never seen.

'What is it? Hip? Knee?'

'It's no big deal. It's nearly healed.'

'What happened?'

'A fall. That's all.'

'Must have been some fall to have taken almost six months to heal.'

The bright smile was fixed in place. At least it looked like a smile, but it felt more as if she was pushing him back with a deadly weapon.

'You know, I've had my fair share of injuries too,' he said, when she didn't reply. 'I played rugby for years. I know that you might never have guessed, thanks to my boyish good looks, but I was a blindside flanker at St Andrew's—when I was at university.'

He tilted his head and showed her the mashed ear that had formed after too many injuries. Luckily that and his broken nose were his only obvious disfigurements, but he'd lost count of the fractures and tears tucked beneath his clothes.

'Blindside flanker...' She looked away, sounding

totally, politely uninterested. 'Sounds like rhyming slang.'

'I was about to be capped for England,' he said, grinning through her cheeky little retort.

'Really?'

At least that merited a second glance. He smiled, nodded, raised his eyebrows. *Got you this time*, he thought.

'About to be? So what happened?'

'Long story. Doesn't matter. So, what exactly is wrong with you, may I ask?'

'It's complicated.'

'I'm sure I'll be able to follow. I've been heavily involved in most sports, one way or another, and I know the pounding bodies take. Ballet is tough—I know that. It might not be my cup of tea, but I respect what you guys do.'

He could see her pausing for a moment, hovering between cutting him off again and continuing the conversation. The smile had dropped and she was watching him carefully, but her body was still coiled tight as a little spring.

'I've not always been a boring old banker. I wasn't born wearing a pinstripe suit,' he said softly. 'Give me a rugby ball any day of the week.'

'So what happened?' she asked. 'Why didn't you follow your dream?'

'Tell me about your injury first,' he countered.

'Cruciate ligament,' she said after a moment.

'Anterior? Posterior? Don't tell me it was one of the collaterals?'

'It was the anterior. I had to have surgery. Twice.'

'Painful,' he said, sucking his teeth. 'You'd better be careful. That can be the end of a beautiful career.'

'I'm well aware of that.'

'I imagine you are. Must be on your mind all the time. One of the players in my uni squad had a terrible time. Had to jack it in eventually. Pity. He had a great future ahead but the injury put paid to all that. I've no idea what he's doing now—he was a bit of a one-trick pony. I don't think he had a Plan B...'

And then suddenly the mask slid down and her brilliant smile slipped and wobbled. Her delicate collarbones bunched and the fine muscles of her throat constricted and closed. She was visibly holding herself in check.

'I'm sorry,' he said. 'That's not what you want to hear right now. Dance is your whole life, isn't it? I totally get it.'

'How can you until it happens to you?'

She shook her head and twisted away from him, staring out over the twinkling yellow lights of London.

'I really do understand,' he said, cringing at his thoughtlessness. 'Rugby was my whole life. As far as I was concerned banking was what my father did. And then—*whoosh*—he died and the carpet got pulled from under my feet. And here I am.'

He looked round at the jet, at the cream leather, the crystal glasses, the plasma screen flashing, the numbers and money, wealth and success. For all the Arturo deal would be the icing on the cake, he still had a pretty rich cake.

Her face told him she was thinking exactly the same thing and he couldn't blame her for that.

'It's not exactly the same, though, is it?' she said, with a note of wistfulness that rang like a bell in his consciousness. 'You had a Plan B. I've got nothing else. Only this. My whole life has been preparing to be a principal dancer. I'm not good at anything except dancing—I barely got myself together to do this.'

She held out the skirts of her dress and looked right into his eyes with such an imploring look that he thought how easy it would be to fall for a woman like her. She was strong, yet vulnerable too—but all he had to do was dive right in and before he knew it he'd be scrabbling for the banks of some fast-flowing river or, worse, being dragged under and losing his mind along the way.

He would not be diving into anything. Arm's length was the only safe distance with any woman— especially one that looked like this—because even when he was crystal-clear it always ended up the same way, with her wanting more than he could give.

Relationships: the rock he was not prepared to perish on again. No way. The skill came in avoiding crashing into that rock by keeping it light, keeping it moving along, keeping it all about the 'now'. Worrying about the future…that wasn't such a great idea.

He turned to Ruby, lifted her chin with his finger, the lightest little touch.

'You're doing a fine job. You've nothing at all to worry about,' he said, hearing himself use his father's gentle but firm *pull yourself together* tone.

But she shook her head and lifted those doe eyes.

'I'm not. I'm useless. I've left the notes I wrote out at home on the table. And I spent hours writing them—in case I forgot something. I can't hold things in my head, other than dance steps, and it's been months since I've danced. I'm terrified that I'll have even forgotten how to do that.'

'Well, one thing at a time, yeah? You've been brilliant so far. I had no idea I was going to see a ballet based on a poem by Rumi, who I used to think was an amazing poet—back when my head was full of mush. Maybe I'll see the error of my ways. Who knows?'

'You really don't mind that I've been a bit of a disaster so far? I don't want to spoil your evening.'

'It's certainly different.'

'You're really going to love the ballet. I promise you.'

She smiled. Wide and fresh and beautiful. He wondered if she knew it was her deadliest weapon. She had to. She might say that she was no good at anything except dancing, but he would wager she could wrap pretty much anyone, male or female, around her little finger with just a flash of that smile or a glance from those eyes.

The plane touched down and rolled along the runway. This was shaping up to be quite an evening—the last before he turned all his attention towards netting Arturo. So he might as well enjoy it.

The game was definitely on.

CHAPTER FOUR

SO, THE LOVE RAT wasn't so much of a rat after all.

He *could* have gone to town on her for messing up with the notes, but he'd let her off the hook and he'd actually been quite kind when she'd almost started blubbing like a baby.

He wasn't just a boring banker. He was smart. And handsome. Even with a broken nose and a flattened ear he was built like a man should be built.

She glanced down at his thighs and his biceps, pushing out the fabric of his tux as they waited in the back of a limousine to take their journey along the red carpet. He was prepped and primed to play the role of patron, and all the doubts she'd felt that he was just a surly shadow of his mother were gone. He could dial up the charm as easily as she could.

Or down. He was no pussycat either. He'd grilled her when he'd first met her, and that had been no party, but she could see why. He was only trying to protect his mother, and who could blame him for that? In his place she'd have been exactly the same—

though of course that was never going to happen. The last person that would need any defending was her mother…except from herself.

The car door was opened. It was time to go. Matteo turned to her, gave her a wink and a smile and stepped out, walking off towards the entrance with lithe grace, light-footed.

It was just like stepping on stage without the dance steps, she thought. Her stomach flipped. She took a breath and popped her smile into place. Then she followed him past the flashing cameras, pausing beside him as he chatted in the foyer, breathing in and out and beaming for all she was worth.

With moments left until curtain up they went on into the auditorium, where the air above the velvet rows bubbled with excitement. Heads turned everywhere as they stepped out into the royal box. Ruby stared straight ahead, the interest of so many people feeling like hives on her skin.

She moved to sit down in the row behind his, but he indicated with a smile and a gracious gesture that she should sit beside him.

He leaned close as the lights dimmed.

'You're sure this is going to be as good as you say?'

'If it isn't you can always ask for your money back.'

The music struck up. A penetratingly beautiful note was sung in the unmistakable voice of an Indian woman, cutting through the atmosphere of the theatre like a sabre through silk. The audience gasped.

Matteo's eyes held hers. A shiver ran down her spine.

'Or I can take recompense another way,' he said.

Slowly his eyes swept over her bare shoulders and décolleté, down to her mouth and then back to her eyes. She felt it in every tiny pore, every nerve, every fibre of her body. His mouth curled into a smile…some promise of what he would take. With each second she felt the charge of attraction flare between them. Her whole body reacted as easily as if he'd flipped a switch. She wasn't imagining it.

She sat back in her seat, blind to the emergence of the principal dancers onto the stage. Some part of her knew that they were dancing—striking buoyant and beautiful poses, their costumes flowing and extending the elegance of each step, the hauntingly beautiful song telling the story of the stirrings of early passion between the dancers—and some part of her watched. But most of her was alive to this totally new sensation.

'Having fun?' he whispered.

Yes, she wanted to gasp out loud. For the first time in months she felt she was actually living. The dance, the theatre, the interested crowd and, despite knowing the dangers, the magnetic draw of this man.

'I'd rather be on stage with them,' she said, for the first time in her life doubting it was actually true.

'I'd love to see you dance.'

He leaned further into her space. His voice, close to her ear, was thrilling. It was that even more than the dance that set her nerves on edge, dancing their own feverish path across her skin.

'I imagine you'd be amazing. Maybe one day...'

For a moment she thought he was going to touch her—his hand hovered and then landed again on his own leg. She stared at it, and then risked a glance to the side, where his profile was outlined in a sleek silver line from the stage lights. He stared straight ahead, rapt, but she could feel something between them, a strange energy that made her suddenly aware of her bare flesh, her braless breasts under the bodice of the dress, her thighs as she crossed and uncrossed her legs, her feet in tiny straps and pointed heels.

Her body was what she used to express herself. It was her language, her vocabulary. She could read and sense others through their wordless actions too. How they held themselves. She could see how nervous or confident they were in the tilt of their head or the curl of their shoulders. And the language he was speaking now was as sensual as any lovers' *pas de deux*. She was aroused by it. She was aroused by him.

She strained forward, facing the stage as the dancers drew pictures of their anguished love, their bodies twisting and writhing with pleasure and pain. And in every move she felt the exquisite pleasure of physical love. And she saw herself with him as the hero lifted his lover and then let her slide down his body, his hands skimming her waist, her ribs, her breasts, before clutching her face and holding it close against his.

She had danced and felt hands on her body—all dancers had—but she had never, ever felt the way she was feeling right now, simply sitting, watching. Waiting.

It was electrifying. And he had to be feeling it too?

'What do you think?' she whispered in a voice not even her own.

'I think I'm hooked—I think I might just have found my newest passion.'

His expressionless face told her nothing, but the effect of his words sent another searing flash of heat to her core. She watched the final scene in the dreamy haze, felt his hand brushing hers, his foot touching hers—tiny little accidental movements that made her skittish.

Finally it ended. There was uproar from the audience, people yelling 'Bravo!' and stamping, up on their feet. She sat there, stunned, beside him. Although she faced forward all her vision was from the corner of her eye—his thigh, his hands clapping in front of his chest, his secret smile as he turned to her.

'So now, I take it, I have to meet the dancers?' he said. 'And then…'

He speared her with a dark look that thrilled her to her core.

She turned back to face the stage, clapping her hands, trusting herself only to stare at the line of dancers taking their bows. He stood beside her as the dancers looked to the royal box. He beamed down at them, waving a salute and applauding once more.

Ruby stood up too. Her legs shook. The theatre lights came up and the crowds began to move. Security appeared, opening the doors and leading them out. She followed Matteo's back, his sure stride, out and down through the theatre to the back of the stage, people parting like waves before them.

Post-performance adrenaline was pulsing through the air as they walked the line-up. Glittering eyes shone through smudged make-up and gleaming, sore bodies. She felt almost as exhilarated as the soloists and principals as she introduced them.

She could see their raised eyebrows and wide-mouthed smiles. She knew they were watching her closely, would be gossiping excitedly. *Ruby the weirdo, who never put a foot out of line, was flirting with the patron.*

Let them. It didn't mean she was going to let herself or anyone else down. She had her head screwed on.

Round the room stood tables laden with drinks and food. She felt a hand on her back, guiding her towards them, and her body tensed and melted. Matteo.

He raised his eyes and smiled indulgently, as if to say, *More delay*, and she had no thirst for the champagne that was thrust into her hand. She could barely concentrate as she tried to resist being buffeted by the waves of her physical attraction to Matteo as close-eyed scrutiny lapped like the tide where she stood.

When he leaned his ear over his right shoulder—a

sign that he wanted more information about someone or something—she happily stood on tiptoe, letting the moments when she whispered names take longer. She lingered there, enjoying the sensation. He placed his hand on her waist, splayed his fingers, tugged her close, and she let her lips brush the side of his cheek.

His skin was soft, but grazed with stubble, and his scent was incredibly subtle. But his aroma, his essence, was magnetic, irresistible male.

'Say that again,' he demanded as she delivered him someone's name. As she tried to pull back a waiter came into view with a wide tray of canapés lifted high on his shoulder. Matteo sidestepped to let him pass and tugged her close to his body. She stood without moving, her breast and hip completely against him, pressed flush. Desire curled—hot and heavy and low in her body.

She knew she should move but she couldn't seem to do anything other than stand with her body against his, loving the mixture of sure, solid sensation and the sweet yearning to feel closer. Blood was rushing all around her, and she was feeling lightheaded as the noise of the party bubbled higher.

People bustled past, but what did she care…?

The waiter passed again and finally they stepped away.

'Who is the blonde woman in green, walking towards us with your director?'

Ruby flicked her eyes away and looked down quickly as a wave of guilt washed over her. Her director had trusted her to show Matteo around. She was the one who had her head screwed on. She couldn't bear it if she disappointed him.

'Dame Cicely Bartlett,' she said, focussing. 'The actress turned politician. She's going to make a political point about under-funding for the arts...'

'I'm impressed. You really *do* know everything about your world. With or without your notes.' He stepped closer to her again. 'Are you all right? You look pale all of a sudden.'

He took her hand in his, rubbed his fingers over the back of her wrist, and words died in her throat. She fought to keep her head from rolling back. She was sick with desire, weaker with every passing moment. She had to stop this before it got out of hand.

'If you don't mind, I think I need to sit down. I've had a bit too much champagne.'

He manoeuvred her into a chair.

'I'm so sorry. What was I thinking? As soon as I've finished with Dame Cicely we can go to supper.'

Supper? He didn't really mean that, did he? He meant sex.

The thought sent her stomach flipping through her ribs. She couldn't go through with this. Who was she trying to kid? She would end up back at his place and then the kissing would start. And then the touching. And then she'd realise that she'd changed her mind. She'd want to get away, then he'd look baffled and wonder what was going on. She'd call a cab and go. It was the way it always ended.

And that would usually be fine because she'd never see them again. But Matteo Rossini was their patron, and she couldn't make a fool of herself with someone like him.

'I don't think that's such a good idea.'

'What's wrong?' he said, stepping close enough for her to see the tiny indentations of his chest hair through the silk of his shirt, the hollow of his strong throat above the collar, the curl of those lips that had grazed her cheek, her jaw, her ear, that she so desperately wanted to feel against her mouth. He stood there and she felt the might and allure of his body pounding down her flimsy defences.

Maybe this time would be different? It felt different…

'Ruby, it's a *very* good idea,' he said softly.

'No, honestly. I'm really tired. I should go home.'

He was scrutinising every inch of her face, staring into her eyes as if he was seeing right inside her head.

'You're not tired. You're nervous. You're worried that people are judging you.'

He nodded, then looked over her shoulder, frowning. 'Wait here. Don't move.'

He moved away and she stood alone in the thinning crowd. She felt as if night had fallen and she was left alone in a moonless sky. She wanted more of him…more of his light.

'Right. That's the bank committed to support Dame Cicely's dance graduate programme. Your director is delighted and he told me to pass that on to you. So my work here is done. We're going for supper and I'm not taking no for an answer.'

The impact of those words lit her up, smashing the last of her resistance.

'OK,' she said. 'Supper would be lovely.'

He took her hand and she didn't pull away. In minutes they were winding through the remains of the throng. People approached with open smiles and hands outstretched to say goodbye and he smiled, shook their hands and smoothly swung past them, patted them on the back and moved on.

The exhilarating rush of what was to come overpowered her every other sensation.

Security men stood at the door, eyeing everything. Matteo nodded as they walked past them, along a passageway and out onto the street. At the car he stopped, turned, gave her the most heart-stopping smile.

'Ready?' he said.

'As I've ever been,' she whispered.

The car door was opened. She slid inside.

CHAPTER FIVE

'CAN'T THIS WAIT, DAVID? I'm right in the middle of something.'

Matteo nodded to the driver to go and lifted Ruby's fingers into his hand. If it wasn't for this call he would have been lifting them to his lips.

'Of course. I can wait until tomorrow morning to tell you that Claudio has approached Augusto Arturo about a merger, if that's what you'd prefer.'

'That's not news. I already knew that. He hasn't a chance.'

He put his arm around Ruby's shoulders, tucking her close, sliding his fingers down her silken flesh as the car rolled through night-time traffic.

'Apparently there's a been a change of heart. They were spotted at lunch in Cannes.'

Matteo's stomach lurched. He sat forward. Lunch meant that they were starting to explore things informally. That was not good news at all.

'What? Are you sure? Where did you find this out?'

'Interestingly, Claudio posted on social media.

Shall I read it to you? *"Looking forward to catching up with old friends and new in the French Riviera this summer. Obligatory Cordon D'Or Regatta and then a weekend in Tuscany with the irrepressible Arturo Augusto."'*

'You've got to be joking. What does he think he's playing at? "Obligatory Cordon D'Or"—he's the last person I want to see there. And name-dropping Augusto? That doesn't prove anything.'

'It proves that he knows how to wind you up.'

Matteo sat as still as his bursting blood vessels and pounding heart would allow. He would *not* over-react to this. He knew Claudio and he knew how he operated. There would be nothing to gain by getting himself in a tailspin over something like this.

'You're right. Claudio knows how important this is to us. It doesn't matter a damn to him if he gets Arturo or not. He doesn't need those clients—it's hardly even worth his while. What do you think he's really up to?'

'In my view, I think he's trying to provoke you. Get you to react to his message. He'll have seen all the recent publicity about you and maybe he thinks you want to play it out publicly. That's my best guess. As you say, turning up at Cordon D'Or would be a new tactic, to say the least. I'll step up security just in case.'

'I didn't see this coming. I really thought he'd have bigger fish to fry.'

The anger he felt was as much anger at himself

for being so damned naïve as at Claudio. He should never have made assumptions about anything involving Claudio Calvaneo. It was if he was determined to erase every last trace of Banca Casa di Rossini and all it stood for.

'That may well still be the case. The only thing we can be sure of is that Banca Casa di Rossini is a much better bet for Arturo than Calvaneo Capital. Even if Claudio decides he wants it, there's no reason to suppose he can make it happen.'

'At best it's his sick little way of needling me. At worst it's the start of a full-blown attempt to merge or buy. Either way, there's nothing I can do about it now.'

'I hope it hasn't ruined your evening, but I thought you'd want to know—just in case.'

Just in case. Matteo knew what that meant. There was a time when he might have done something stupid—he'd have given his right arm to do something stupid, to see Claudio sprawled out in front of him, begging for mercy, to see him confessing his crimes, to see any kind of justice at all.

But it wouldn't happen that way. He knew his physical strength—and his weaknesses. He could take Claudio out with one punch. But then where would they be? With him in jail—his mother's biggest fear. He'd grudgingly had to accept that it was possible, and had stayed well away for years.

But now this? His gut was telling him that soon they would be coming face to face in the showdown that would decide the fate of Banca Casa di Rossini. And Claudio was going to play it out like a boxing match—making cheap gibes to goad him.

He had to rein it in, bide his time, keep his head clear.

'Thanks, David. I appreciate that. I'll sleep on it. Let's catch up tomorrow.'

He sat back, his mind racing as it always did whenever Claudio butted his way back into his life. But he had to get it into perspective. There was nothing he could do until he met with Augusto Arturo himself. He couldn't control who the old man had lunch with. He could only control himself.

'Is everything all right?'

He looked round. Ruby stared at him with wide, almond eyes.

'Absolutely, sweetheart.'

If there was anything at all that was going to help him get through the next twenty-four hours it was this woman. He was going to give them both a night to remember.

'Just work. Nothing for us to trouble ourselves over.'

'Hmm…if you say so.'

'I say so,' he said. He reached for her. 'I've got to keep my phone beside me, but I don't think we'll be disturbed now. And here we are…'

The car rolled to a halt outside Luigi's, one of his favourite restaurants, where the food was amazing and the staff were fast and friendly.

He got out and stood on the pavement, rolled his tensed shoulders and willed himself to clear his mind. He breathed deeply, inhaling the sultriness of the evening, the dense, heady scent of the jasmine planted on either side of the restaurant entrance.

Ruby emerged from the car. Just looking at her was like a sip of summer wine, full of promise, easing him into a better place.

He hoped.

Just one more detail to be sure of before he could completely relax with her...

Minutes later they were settled in a subtly lit corner of the restaurant, where shadows licked at Ruby's delicate throat, her fine-boned chest and long slim arms as they rested on the white tablecloth. He so badly wanted to reach across the table and take hold of her hand, trail his fingers along her collarbone, absorb the softness of her skin.

But control was all. Control and then controlled release. Like exercising a muscle.

'You were amazing tonight,' he said. 'I couldn't have asked for a better assistant. You know your world inside out and you didn't need any notes. I'm impressed.'

'It's easy when it's something you care about.'

'It's not just dance, is it? You care about the company, too. It's obvious how much those people mean to you.'

He thought of her face, shining with pride as she

introduced him to her colleagues, how they'd embraced and smiled happily together.

'They've been my family for years. I've been very lucky.'

'You mean that in a figurative sense, of course?'

'I mean that since the age of eleven I've been with the British Ballet as a boarder. So they really are my family. My mum and her boyfriend moved to the south coast when I was twelve, but I was able to stay here. I'm in with the bricks,' she said brightly, ending the sentence with a fake note of joy.

He was beginning to recognise her little signatures: the overly bright smile, the wide-eyed stare, the *happy to help* tone in her voice. Those little idiosyncrasies could pull a man under if he wasn't careful.

'I'm sure everything will work out for you, Ruby,' he said. 'Even if it's not performing on the stage there must be other things you can do with the company—assuming you want to stay with them? Education or... I don't know, maybe you want to see a bit more of the world? Aren't there jobs in other companies?'

'Of course there are, but I'm not exactly in a position to plan anything yet. It all depends on what my consultant says next month.'

'And if you get the all-clear would you move? Is there anything—or anyone—holding you here?'

'I don't have anyone special in my life if that's what you mean?'

'That's exactly what I mean.'

She screwed up her face. 'My track record with men isn't exactly my strong suit. I've never been much for socialising, and this injury has completely drained me—so, no, there's no one special in my life.'

'My track record with women isn't exactly *my* strong suit either.'

Her lips curled into a mocking smile. 'For completely different reasons.'

'So the press would have you believe,' he said, grateful for the arrival of the waiters. He didn't particularly want to go into any of his relationship back story with her. Nor did he want to know hers. Sharing all that stuff gave out the wrong signals—as if he cared, as if there was going to be a future between them.

They sat silently at the circular table, watching as napkins were flicked and laid over their laps, as platters of cheese and meat, olives and artichokes and glistening melon were laid down and wine sloshed gaily into their glasses.

All the while her eyes widened, and in the candlelight the hollows of her cheeks seemed to deepen and the column of her throat lengthen as she sat forward to stare at each plate.

Finally the waiters bowed and left.

'Tuck in,' he said, steepling his fingers and watching as she began to eat, cutting cubes of melon and ham slowly at first, swallowing delicately, then devouring them and washing it down with sips of wine.

It satisfied something deep within him that he was able to provide food for her. He'd taken dozens of women to dinner, and never once before had he ever taken such pleasure in watching anyone eat. She was fresh and new and lovely and she didn't care about what the all the others cared about. She hadn't shown any interest in the jet or the car, or the people who clambered all over him to get their picture taken. She genuinely wanted to make him like the ballet and the dancers. She cared.

He knew that feeling. It was buried deep inside him. The passion for his game, the hunger to train and win. The drive to get better and better and then the ultimate payback: the chance to play for his country.

He would never forget that soaring feeling of joy when the coach had pulled him aside and told him he was under consideration. He hadn't even told his parents—only Sophie. She'd been the only one he'd trusted, the only one who had known what it meant to him.

But that was all in the past now. Even if he hadn't had the heart ripped out of him, he was never going to be able to dedicate himself to rugby again. Not with a widowed mother and a bank to pull back from the brink. His family pride as well as billions in sterling, euros and Swiss francs were in the balance. There was no possible way he could turn his back on that and run out onto a muddy field.

Sometimes money sickened him. Greed climbed

inside people's souls and turned them black. Like Claudio. The man had always been rich in his own right, but he wanted even more than money. And look where that had got them all.

He looked up to see Ruby sitting back from the table with a happy, sated smile.

'Is that better?'

She beamed, revealing her dimples to him. 'Oh, yes, thank you. It was delicious.'

'That was just the starter. You've got space for more?' he asked as the table was cleared and re-stocked with all sorts of sharing plates of pasta, fish and salad.

'Maybe a little,' she said, her eyes widening over the next load of steaming dishes. 'I don't normally eat a lot. Well, that's not strictly true—I normally stuff my face. But not recently. Not since I've not been able to dance.'

'Don't they pay you?' he asked. 'Don't they see you as an investment?' It was none of his business but the injustice of it puzzled him.

'Of course they look after me—but if I can't dance I can't dance.'

She turned her head to the side and twirled her ponytail through her fingers.

'Anyway, all you need to know is that I've been on a bit of a tight budget recently. Normally I'd pay my share if I was on a date, but I'm a bit broke until my cheque clears.'

'Is this a date, Ruby?'

The forkful of pasta she had stabbed and was drawing up to her open mouth was placed down carefully. She looked up and the flickering candlelight licked the hollows of her huge almond eyes. He didn't think he'd ever seen a more beautiful woman.

'I... I don't think so.'

'We've already established that there's something interesting going on between us. Wouldn't you agree?'

'Is this how you normally seduce women?' she asked. 'I thought you'd be a bit more subtle.'

She picked up her cutlery again and continued eating, her eyebrows raised like two black birds, mocking him. He couldn't help but smile at her quick-on-the-draw retort, but he wasn't going to let her off that easily.

'I didn't think we were working on the premise of "subtle". I thought you were quite clear that you found me sexually attractive.'

She put her hand to her chest. The solid line of her dress cut right across the shadows of her small breasts and his eyes fell there. She was exquisite. And he allowed himself the luxury of imagining what those small breasts looked like, what those rosy nipples would taste like rolling under his tongue.

'What? You're shocked that I would call you on that?'

'I'm shocked at your double standards. *You're* the one who's been putting it out all night.'

'Ha! Oh, really?'

'Absolutely. Every time I had to say something to you, you were well inside my personal space. I couldn't move so much as an inch and you were right beside me, hands all over me.'

'Is that right? Hands all over you?' He could barely contain his chuckle. She was making him more and more aroused with every second. 'Well, I have to apologise. I didn't notice you pulling away or asking me to back out of your "personal space". In fact, as I recall, in between your breathy little whispers, you liked to linger in *my* personal space much longer than a person would normally take to move away. In fact I'd go so far as to say you were almost rubbing yourself against me. Maybe that's something that you dancers think is normal, but for the rest of us—I'd say that that was provocative.'

As he spoke he watched her face react. Her eyes widening and the trouble she was having swallowing. It was pure, unadulterated pleasure—just what he needed.

'That was *you*! You were provoking me!'

'And I happen to know just how sensitive your ears and neck are.'

He looked there now, watching the soft pink flush that was travelling all over her cheeks, imagining how she was going to react the next time he touched her.

'You could barely stay upright when I had to ask you a question. If I brought my lips anywhere close to your ear you practically melted in my arms. You have a very responsive erogenous zone.'

She rolled her eyes, as if he was talking rubbish, but she couldn't disguise her smile or the deepening of her blush. She was playing for time, and every second thickened the hot, heavy, sultry air between them.

'I was only doing my job,' she said, looking up at him coyly. 'It's not my fault if you read more into it than was actually there.'

'Ah. I *see*. I was imagining things.' He knew women. He knew what he was and wasn't imagining. 'I'd certainly like to revisit my poor judgement over dessert. If I'm wrong, you'll have my full apology. If I'm right...'

'We'll see,' she said, and she gave a tiny shrug, the twin hollows of her perfect collarbones softly shadowed in candlelight.

But with each second he could see her reaction deepen. He could feel it. Unless he was completely off his game, this was shaping up to be a night to remember.

He leaned forward and took her hand, secretly thrilled when she didn't try to pull away. He traced the fine veins that lay across her wrist, circled them over and over with his thumb. Her eyelids fluttered and her lips parted.

'Indeed we will.'

He brought her fingers to his lips softly, gently. Her eyelids dropped. He smiled and ran his fingers up and down the smooth skin of her forearm. She was visibly melting under his touch, but still she held something back.

'I missed an evening at the casino tonight, but I'm willing to bet that I'll have discovered every last one of your erogenous zones before dawn.'

'I'd better warn you: I'm not really into sex,' she breathed through a heavy-lidded smile.

He tipped her face towards him until her mouth was at the perfect angle. He looked into her eyes, and in that moment he saw the wariness of the little girl she must once have been, but quickly it was gone and desire swept her lids closed.

He angled his mouth and placed one slow, soft kiss on her lips. And then he slowly drew back.

'That lengthens the odds, but I'm still willing to take the risk.'

A smile broke across her full, kissable lips. Her eyes opened slowly.

'You're on,' she said.

CHAPTER SIX

RUBY STEPPED OUT onto the terrace and walked to the wall that separated Matteo's penthouse apartment from the rest of the dazzling London skyline. Below her the glow of a thousand lamps lit up the Thames embankment. Boats glided this way and that on the mottled surface of the river, which rolled along under a clear night sky.

A tiny light breeze wafted over her bare skin and she touched her arms, holding herself close. She looked at the champagne flute, half full and balanced on the wall, and listened again for the sound of Matteo's voice, rumbling low within the apartment—the third call he'd had to take this evening so far.

The life of a corporate exec.

She'd had no idea that people lived like this, in surroundings like this, on call day and night, and for a moment she let herself imagine becoming part of it. The money, the views, the parties. The meetings in boardrooms with demanding clients and hungry shareholders. She imagined him delivering a presentation in a glass-walled office, all eyes watching him, thought how impressive he must be in his world. How different that world was from hers.

The shadowy shape-shifting future that she'd always imagined only ever featured herself—alone. It was a world on-stage, pushing herself to her limits, twisting her body into the shapes that she had practised over and over in rehearsal, presenting to one audience after another, relishing their thrilled excitement and basking in their awe as they rose to their feet, applauding.

There was never any 'afterwards'. No handsome husband to share the cab ride home with. No children waiting to say goodnight with the nanny, sleepy-eyed and pink-cheeked. No mother on the phone gushing with pride.

She'd never seen those things in her future, and until this moment she had never even known they might be missing. Her dream had been the same since the moment she could remember. Since her first ballet lessons at the church hall and the surprised pleasure of the teacher, telling her mum that her daughter was *'very talented'*. She'd danced everywhere she went—the bus stop, in the supermarket—and people had beamed at her, filling up that achy dark spot inside her with their happy smiles.

She would turn to her mother, expecting to see the same happiness, but it had hardly ever been there. She had been deep in her own world, her mobile phone never far away, her own heart broken and never healing. Not until she'd met George. And then it had all been decided.

In her mind it had felt like coming to the top of a road and seeing two paths going in totally different directions. The promise of a 'new life' in Cornwall, with Mum and George. New school, new friends. She would still dance. They did ballet in Cornwall for goodness' sake. But Ruby had known—she had known what that new life would really be like. It would be all about George. There would be no dance—not like she'd had before—and there would be even less of her mother's love...

She snapped out of her memories as Matteo finished his call and walked across the wooden floor. Her heart began to skip and her stomach flipped again against her ribs. He had been the perfect gentleman since they'd left the restaurant. Faultless. *Too* faultless. Attentive and caring and kind. He'd asked after her knee...asked was she still hungry? Could he prepare her some food? Bring her some wine? Could he kiss her here and here?

He paused in the doorway, his white shirt unbuttoned at the neck and the dark shadow of hair and muscle excruciatingly close and alluringly touchable. Once again she felt that deep tug in her core. But she didn't fight it—she couldn't. The battle was well and truly lost.

'I'm sorry about that,' he said, walking up to her and circling his arm around her waist.

He delivered another soft, leisurely kiss to her lips

and then pulled back and smiled at her. Just as he'd done several times already in the past hour.

'I hope you don't mind. But that should be the end of it until tomorrow morning.'

'I guess there's never any real downtime in your world. There's always someone's needs to take care of. High net worth people must be very high maintenance.'

'You're right. And I can't pretend that that's my favourite part of the job. You know, in the summer I'll be on the Riviera most weekends? We host a regatta for charity. All the big names come. Sounds amazing, yes? But it'll be full-on. Entertaining can be draining.'

'Yes—so I witnessed tonight.'

'But you were the best possible antidote,' he said, leaning in for another kiss. 'I'd never have thought I'd hear myself saying I had a great time at the ballet. But I did. He tugged her close and started to trail kisses on her neck. 'Thanks to you…'

Once again she felt herself melt into his arms, felt those overwhelming urges rise up within her. She turned around in his arms, aching to feel his lips on her mouth, his hands on her body, but every time she thought he was going to finally lead her off to bed he cooled them down again—like the conductor of an orchestra, setting the beat and the heat of their passion.

She'd never had an experience like it.

He walked to the wine bucket and lifted the champagne bottle, topped up her glass and handed it to her, looked around for his own. The tray of *petits-fours* and strawberries lay untouched. She sipped the champagne, but truly she only had an appetite for Matteo now.

'What do you think of the view?' he said, leaning beside her. 'Isn't it spectacular? I never tire of this city. Even Rome doesn't do it for me the way that London does. And Rome is in my blood.'

He hooked his arm around her shoulders as they stared down at the river. Two party boats, illuminated and booming with the deep bass sounds of dance music, sailed past one another in opposite directions, while on the bridges above them traffic rumbled back and forth.

'Honestly? I've never seen the city from up high before. This is a totally different place from the London I know. Even though we're only a few miles apart. You see those buses down there? That's usually me on one of them, while you're up here—or up there. Do you have one of those?'

She pointed at a helicopter hovering above the roof of a nearby tower block.

'Not at the moment, no. But where is your world? Can you see it from here? Show me.'

He circled his arm around her waist once more and laid his hand on the wall, tucking her close to his body.

'Way over there is Croydon. That's where I grew

up. Before Mum moved away and I became a boarder at the British Ballet.'

She paused, expecting him to ask her for more details. It was a subject of great interest to most people—how her mother had moved three hundred miles away with her boyfriend and started a new family, conveniently forgetting the child she already had. She barely understood it herself, but she didn't blame her mother.

She'd started with good intentions, but it had all fallen apart after a year or so. There had been visits and phone calls during which Ruby had forced herself not to cry. Because she had known that if she'd cried she'd have had to leave ballet school and move to Cornwall. And be eclipsed there for ever, in the shadow of George and the twins that were about to be born.

They were sixteen now, she thought suddenly. Sixteen—almost adults themselves—and still no sign that she was ever going to get along with them. The awful thing was she just didn't *feel* anything for them. It was terrible to admit it, even if only to herself. Was it because they didn't look like her? They had their mother's blonde hair, George's sturdy build, while she was dark, slight...

She looked out across the river, at the moonless sky, the endless inky horizon. Somewhere out there she had family who looked like her. Uncles, aunts, cousins. Brothers, sisters. People with features like hers, minds like hers. Maybe dancers like her...

Her mind conjured up her favourite daydream. She was dancing on some foreign stage—the performance of her life. A man stood in the audience—her father. He called her name, pushed forward to see her, She shielded her eyes and then she saw him. *'Father,'* she cried...

Her heart leapt into her throat and her eyes burned. Beside her, Matteo moved closer and she tensed. For a moment she was still lost on that dark stage, searching for that face.

'You must have been a very gifted child,' said Matteo through her dream.

She felt his fingers cradle the back of her head. She let her head rest there, grateful for the warmth, the strength, the masculine grasp. She didn't fight it. Emotions were surfacing tonight that she'd kept buried for a long, long time. Maybe it was the champagne. Maybe it was the soft touch of his fingers on her skin, being held close...

She turned in his arms. Another kiss—gentle, soft. The slide of his tongue dipping into her mouth. She accepted it gratefully, eagerly. He pressed closer, his arms encircling her at the wall.

'Something like that,' she said on a sigh, relieved to be pulled from her memories as her head fell back and the ache between her legs grew hotter and heavier.

'I really can't wait to see you dance,' whispered Matteo as he hooked his other arm around her and drew her into his sensual world.

He placed tiny little kisses on her neck, which had her extending her head to give him more access. She sighed and shifted against him and he pulled her closer, his hands holding her possessively. She relaxed against his broad, strong chest and felt the urgent ridge of his desire. His kisses travelled to her ear and she shivered as a huge spasm of desire ricocheted through her.

'Matteo, please...' she moaned.

'You like this, don't you?' he murmured. 'Your secret exogenous zone. And we still have all the others to find too, before dawn.'

He kissed her again, nibbled and suckled at the edge of her earlobe, licked and kissed and nuzzled her neck. She was tired of holding back. Tired of striving so hard for so long and there being nothing to show for it. She was tired of feeling hungry for life, of starving herself of pleasure, fun. She'd worked so hard to get here and the exhaustion of keeping it together was lapping inside her now like the relentless dragging of the tide.

Her own private rules—training and abstinence, working until her body was exhausted to be the best, to please—had been her whole life as far back as she could remember, with little time to relax because it was too terrifying to stop.

She deserved this night. She needed it.

Under her dress her nipples throbbed in tight buds and she felt almost unbearably aroused. She pressed even closer to his body, the full skirt of her dress swishing noisily as she ached to feel his lips on her mouth and his hands on her body.

He held her head in his hands, kissing her mouth until it opened, his tongue plundering deeply inside. She kissed him back and pressed herself closer, desperate to free herself from all this red froth, to step out of it naked and feel his hands on her body.

She wanted to feel the way she knew he could make her feel.

'The bet's off. Take me to bed,' she breathed.

The words spilled from her mouth into the hot heavy air between them and he stopped. She looked up into those chestnut eyes, willing him to take control now that she had relented. Willing him to do what she trusted him to do—give her the oblivion she sought.

She reached up and traced her finger around his mouth, feeling the graze of stubble, the soft pad of his lips, then she slid her fingers inside his wet mouth. Her head fell back as he sucked her fingers.

'Exactly what I plan to do.'

He took her hand and led them back indoors, past the discarded champagne and the twin palms on either side of the French doors, nodding in the breeze like benevolent sentries. In through the lounge, where her clutch lay like a red silk flag against one dark leather couch, and where its reflection, his red tie, lay across another. Her skirt swished brazenly with every step she took.

Through an open doorway she glimpsed a solitary

silver bowl, overflowing with fruit—the only sign of life in a gleaming, sterile kitchen. In the shadowy hallway a wall of photographs faced another bare of anything other than lamplight. She caught the face of his mother, smiling on the prow of a yacht, her hair blowing in the sea breeze, and felt a momentary jab of discomfort, a whiff of disloyalty that made her footsteps falter.

He must have sensed it for he turned and caught her eye, holding her steady with his gaze. He cupped her jaw and placed a hot, demanding kiss on her mouth. She felt the brand of his desire.

He walked to a door and opened it into a bedroom. *His* bedroom. Acres of pale carpet spread out under rugs and various pieces of furniture, lit only by the spill of lamplight from either side of a wide, low bed.

She stepped inside. This was it. This was where she was going to be seduced.

Her heart thundered in her chest as she looked around, and there in the mirror Matteo stretched out an arm towards her.

'I've been admiring your dress all night,' he said as he trailed a finger along her collarbone. 'Wondering what you looked like under all this...'

His finger traced the line of her bodice from left to right, lightly brushing the skin of her décolletage. She shivered uncontrollably and closed her eyes as he traced the line down the middle of her chest to where the skirt of the dress flared out. Then he placed a hand on either side of her waist and pulled her towards him for a kiss.

Kiss me and never stop, she thought, loving the sensation of his tongue expertly licking and probing, stoking the fire higher. How could she have denied herself this pleasure…so much pleasure?

Her own greedy fingers pressed against his chest. She could feel the spring of hair under her palms and rubbed tiny circles there, loving the sensation of his firm muscle, loving the groans of pleasure she was making him deliver.

Fumbling, she undid his shirt all the way down to the waist, until the twin panels of fabric opened to reveal a golden chest dusted with hair that narrowed down into a single dark line, swallowed up by the waistband of his trousers. She pulled the shirt from his trousers, her eye landing for a moment on the huge hard ridge at his groin, and she bit back a groan of anticipation.

She had seen countless male bodies—men at the peak of physical fitness, slick with sweat and shaved clean of hair. But none of them had proclaimed their masculinity like Matteo as she pushed his shirt from his shoulders and drank in the sight of his magnificent naked torso.

She bit her lip and then looked up at him, smiling a dark, devilish smile.

'What's going through your dirty little mind?' he whispered, leading her to the bed and pulling her down on top of him.

She pulled her skirt up round her waist and sat back on her heels, straddling him. 'You,' she said, rocking slightly back and forth.

His erection throbbed between her legs in response. Her panties were thin and the sensation of his arousal was almost too much to bear. She rocked against him again. It felt heavenly. He watched her closely, and the thrill of seeing him and feeling him sent wave after wave of pleasure through her.

But as he reached his hands up to touch her she stilled his wrists. 'Don't move,' she said.

She closed her eyes and rubbed again. She was *so* close to orgasm.

'Please don't move.'

He didn't move a muscle but he grew harder.

'You dirty, dirty girl.'

She stared down at him…at every gorgeous masculine inch of him She rocked again, staring into his eyes.

'You want me to lie here between your legs and not get to touch you, but you can pleasure yourself against me until you come? Is that what's going on here?'

She threw her head back and rubbed harder.

She felt his hands close around her arms. 'There will be hell to pay for this, Ruby.'

'Yes—yes!' she cried, rubbing herself harder still.

In the quiet of the night she could hear the rustle of her dress and feel the friction of her bare feet on the smooth cotton sheets. And she heard the sounds of their flesh touching, hot and wet and insistent. And his breath. And his passion. And the knowledge that she could do this.

'Come for me Ruby. *Now*.'

And she did.

The huge, hot orgasm burst forth, and she was aware of him lying there, telling her to keep coming.

Then she collapsed on his chest. His heart was pounding. A cry had died somewhere in her throat. His hands soothed her back, coiled round her hair, and then in a heartbeat he had flipped her over.

'Glad I could be of some assistance there. And, now, if you don't mind…'

His fingers hooked around her back and instantly found the top of the zip. With one hand he tipped up her chin and held her gaze, and with the other he slowly drew down the zip, all the way to the waist-band.

Then he bent forward, kissed her lips, and with a final tug pulled the dress all the way down. She lay there, warm in her post-orgasm glow, naked apart from her black panties and her shameless desire. And it felt good. It felt wonderful to know how much he was loving her body and how much she was loving his.

'You know you're even more beautiful than I imagined,' he whispered, unfastening his trousers and slipping them off.

The sight of him sent flames dancing all over her

skin. She reached up to touch him but he grabbed at her wrists and gently pushed her down.

'Oh, no. It's my turn now.'

In seconds she was warm in his arms as his head dipped to place kisses on her mouth and then in a trail down the centre of her chest. Her back arched as she thrust her aching breasts forward, desperate to feel his lips there.

'Please, Matteo...' she breathed, staring down at his dark head outlined against her white skin.

He looked straight at her with devilish intent, holding his mouth in place for long, excruciating seconds as she tried to jerk her breast towards him.

'Now, now...you've got to learn patience,' he said, and smiled as he held her fast and then finally, slowly, brought his mouth down to hover over one pink nipple, his tongue dipping low until he finally closed his lips around it and tugged.

'Yes...' she breathed, her eyes scrunched up with pleasure, her back arching further towards him. 'Yes...'

'Oh, yes,' he whispered into her flesh.

He teased and tugged and suckled her nipple until he'd had enough and then moved to the other. Instantly the cool air clenched around her damp skin and she looked down, held his head in place as he drew more and more pleasure from her with his lips.

In seconds he'd scooped his hands under her shoulders and lifted her gently further back onto the bed. 'Do I have to be careful with your knee?' he whispered. 'I can't hurt you, can I?'

She shook her head vigorously. 'Only if you throw me across the room or drop me.'

'I don't plan on that. I've got much better ideas.'

'Like what?' she breathed, loving the way he was dipping his head to take care of one throbbing pink nipple and then the other in quick succession.

'You've got too many clothes on,' he said, kissing his way down to her navel, putting his hands under her bottom and holding her up like some sort of precious object.

'I'm a feminist,' she said, hooking her hands around his neck and pulling him down on top of her. 'What's good for you is good for me.'

'You *are* strong, aren't you?' He smiled, circling her arm in his hand. 'I probably wouldn't mess with you.'

'We can arm wrestle later,' she said as she ran her hands over the satiny skin of his back and down to his shorts and began to tug them off. 'Let's have more fun first.'

But before she could grip them he'd rolled her onto her back and they were kissing. And kissing. And kissing.

More than anything else she wanted to feel every inch of him. With expert hands he pulled off her pants and his, and reached into his bedside table for a condom. She lay back on the bed watching as he held himself in his hand. He was long and thick, and she bit her lip with longing.

'Open your legs for me.'

His voice was almost hoarse, and she could see just how close to the edge he already was.

She lay back and stared at the ceiling, feeling the seconds slip past, but he was there, cradling her in his arms as he moved her exactly where he wanted her. Then, with his lips on hers and his hands on either side of her head, he positioned himself and slid deep inside her.

CHAPTER SEVEN

RUBY WOKE IN the night. She was in a strange bed, in a strange room, and every single fibre of her body tensed in alarm. She was in complete darkness, silent apart from the breathing near her face, Matteo's breathing.

Matteo Rossini, CEO of Banca Casa di Rossini, Love Rat, sponsor of the British Ballet. The last man on earth she should be lying beside.

What had she done? What on earth had she done? How had she ended up here in his bed?

Her mind sped through the events of the night, landing on the moments that had led to this. There had been too much emotion, too many memories unwrapped and unravelled. Far too much champagne and wine. Definitely that was to blame.

She tried to remember how many glasses she'd had. Two? Maybe three? Half a glass when she'd got here?

Was it really the booze that had done for her?

This felt worse than any hangover.

There wasn't any point in lying to herself.

She should never have agreed to stay the night. She felt as if she'd given something away that she'd never get back—let the genie out of the bottle, let herself down. She knew the other dancers thought she was weird because she made a point of setting herself apart. But it wasn't because she thought she was better. It was because she was afraid she was worse...

She had to get out of here—*now*. She couldn't face herself, never mind anyone else.

But suddenly the strong, heavy weight of his arm landed on her waist.

The urge to roll over and slide out of bed was almost unbearable, but she didn't move. She lay still. She had to stop and think—not bolt for the door.

Waking up in a man's bed was not the worst thing in the world. Other people did it.

But his arm was so heavy and he was so close. She could scent their night together—feral and musky. She breathed deeply, feeling her chest fill with air and then slowly empty. What a night. She'd done things she'd never done...feeling and giving pleasure until she had fallen into a deep sleep.

And hadn't he been every bit as amazing a lover as she had thought he would be? And considerate. And kind. She didn't have much to compare him with, of course, but she knew that she'd never been made to feel this way before.

The memory of him finding his release inside her sent echoes of pleasure pulsing through her body and she gave an involuntary sigh. Beside her, Matteo gave a sleepy grunt in response, and once more she had to stifle the urge to move.

Why was she like this? Why couldn't she just lie there in a post-orgasmic glow like everybody else and enjoy it? There was something wrong with her— she knew that. She'd been told by both the men she'd slept with. She could have sex—just about—but staying the night was a complete no-no, and had been the undoing of each of her previous relationships.

I need to get an early night. Her get-out clause of every situation.

But to slope off out of Matteo's bed? After what they'd shared that seemed—*wrong*.

In the darkness of the room gloomy shapes began to form and make sense—a chair here, a table with the round glass vase, the edge of a huge photograph of an island.

The slash of light from below the doorway spilled a silvery glow onto the discarded clothes on the floor. She could just make out the scarlet dress where it lay draped over a chair, its stiff petticoats giving it an air of waiting impatiently to be worn again.

She had enjoyed wearing it last night. Had had so many compliments about how it suited her. But when was she likely to wear a dress like that again?

Matteo would be off soon, back to Rome—more hosting, more guests, more fancy clothes and fancy people.

Her mind wandered, imagining how he would look, what he would wear and who he would meet.

Lady Faye and others like her.

She racked her brains. Had he mentioned her or any of his exes last night? She didn't think so. He hadn't really said much about himself at all. Only the stuff about rugby. He hadn't mentioned any women and had closed her down fast when she'd mentioned his mother.

But all those women in his life, said a little voice. That wasn't such a great character trait. And those were only the ones who'd been photographed. There were bound to be even more—the one-night stands. And now she was one of them...

A sickly sense of unease rolled through her. She could be lying in exactly the same place as countless women before her. That was not a good feeling.

Matteo groaned quietly. He was coming closer to the surface. But if she lay still he might go back under, and then she could slip away—no small talk, no awkward glances, no shame.

His breathing steadied and deepened again and she took her chance, easing out from under his arm, sliding one leg out into the cool of the room, then another, gently shifting her weight, pausing to make sure his breathing hadn't shifted, then easing out further.

Finally she put one leg down on the floor and backed away from the bed and his sleeping form. She felt over the carpet for her shoes, grabbing them up into her hands, then taking her dress from the chair.

She tiptoed across the room, put her hand on the door and eased it open, pausing suddenly when it began to squeak. But Matteo's slow, steady breathing carried on as daylight pushed forward, letting her slip out into the hallway.

She needed to phone a cab and get out of there as quickly as possible. She pulled the door open and paced along the wooden floor, past the photographs of skiing trips and yachting trips, past his mother's beaming face and along the hallway to the kitchen.

There was her bag, and there through the glass was the ice bucket, the strawberries, and her wrap discarded over a chair. Midnight's debris dressed in daylight's accusing glow.

She tugged open the patio door and lifted her bag—but when she turned there was Matteo, framed in the kitchen doorway, tall and bronzed and looking murkier than the Thames on a winter's day.

'Hey,' he said, and his voice was a growl, rough with lack of sleep. 'You're up already.'

He tugged at the waist of his boxers as he walked into the room and she watched as his fingers trailed along the red, raw-looking marks on his stomach. Marks that she had made with her nails.

She looked away. 'Yes. I thought I'd get going. I've got a lot to do.'

He was at the sink. She heard the tap running and the sound of water filling a glass.

'You should have said,' he said, drinking thirstily. 'Could have set an alarm. Want some?'

He wiped water from his mouth with the back of his hand and it was completely mesmerising. Just looking at him made her mouth water, but she shook her head and turned her face away.

'No, thanks. Just call me a cab, please.'

He filled a pot with coffee and water and set it on the hob, looking at her over his shoulder as he did so.

'A cab?' he said. 'You don't want to stay for breakfast? I can order whatever you like. You had a great appetite last night…'

'I'm in a bit of a rush.'

At that he looked up. His eyes flashed with something, but it was too fast to see what before his face smoothed out into rock.

'I didn't catch on to that last night—apologies. I'll not keep you back if you want to go.'

'Yes, I should have said I had to leave early—sorry.'

'It's no problem.'

He paused, and the silence and his accusing stare were like a toxic cloud, mushrooming between them. She tried to find words—but what could she say? It was like corpsing on stage. Sentences were dying in her mind, not even making it to her mouth.

Please let me off the hook, she thought. *Let me go.*

'I thought we had a lovely night, Ruby,' he said finally. 'An amazing night.'

'Yes, we did. Thanks.'

He put his hands up.

'*"Thanks"?* I'm not completely clear what's happening here. I thought we might hang out a bit longer?'

He walked towards her, stretched his hands out as if to rest them on her shoulders. She side-stepped that neatly.

She stared down at a corner of the kitchen worktop along which his mail was arranged in two neat rows. Bills and official-looking stuff in one, and cards and invitations to parties in another. She could see his name emblazoned on one in cursive font and the name of the world-famous hotel it was to be held in. He was probably out every night of the week at some thing or other. Meeting women...having supper afterwards.

That bed was probably never cold.

She turned. Looked at him. At the navy stretch of his boxer shorts as they cut across his perfect stomach, the bump of each muscle and the dark arrow of hair. His wide, hard chest, its bones extending out, broken and uneven on one side, perfect on the other. The wide trunk of his neck, his stubbled jaw, hair messed up and framing his cool morning-after face.

For a split second she hovered. The urge to jump into his arms and wrap her legs around his waist, to bury herself in all that man, glory in the kissing and hugging and sweet, dirty loving they had shared was as tempting as her next breath.

But she didn't move a muscle. Because she

couldn't unwrap herself all over again. She'd get away with it once, but not another time. Not now that she had bound herself back together again.

She shook her head vigorously.

'I can't. I have to go. I'm sorry—I need to…to get things done.'

He was looking at her carefully, warily, and then he put his hands down. 'Fair enough. You don't need to explain anything. I've got a lot on too.'

'Yes, I hope it goes well. So, can you call me a cab, please?'

He looked at her, then lifted his phone. 'Send the car,' he said.

He stared at her, his brown berry eyes now glassy and hard. The coffee brewing on the hob began to splutter and spill out of the spout.

'It won't be too long.'

The lid of the coffee pot rose up as steam and coffee broke free. Matteo reached for it and casually lifted it to the side.

'I can wait downstairs.'

'If you like.'

She strode through the hallway, her heels clicking on the tiles, the faces on the walls grinning like clowns now, mocking her desperation to get out of the apartment, onto the street and out of this stupid dress.

She stared at her scarlet reflection in the hallway mirror, and the agony of waiting was accompanied by the sonorous bell as the lift slowly climbed closer.

'Wait,' said a voice, and then Matteo too was in the mirror, hopping towards her, pulling on a pair of joggers, his big body loose and powerful, his face smooth, his lips closed.

The lift doors opened and she rushed gratefully inside, willing the doors to close before he could come in. But in he came, utterly consuming the air, the space, her line of sight—everything.

She stared straight ahead at their twin reflections, blurred lines in the glass: her in last night's dress and him broad, bronzed and bare-chested.

She bowed her head. 'You don't need to do this.'

'I'll see you into the car.'

The rest of the trip down thirty floors was silent but for the whoosh of the lift. She stared at her shoes. The satin toe of one was scuffed. His feet beside hers were bare. She turned her head.

With infinite slowness the lift finally bumped to a stop and the doors eased open. She stepped out into the plush, hushed reception area. Ahead, the glass doors screened the city—the world she knew, the world she was desperate to reclaim. Anywhere but here.

'This doesn't feel right,' he said, suddenly grabbing her hand. 'This doesn't feel right at all. Did I say something? Or do something?'

They were almost at the doors. A round glass table laden with fruit stood in their way. A car rolled into view.

He swung her round and she looked up into his

face. She memorised the lines of his eyelids, the crooked bridge of his nose, the soft pillow of his lower lip. She'd never see them again.

'I'm sorry,' she said. 'You're just not my type.'

He winced as if she'd slapped him and stepped back.

A doorman loomed into sight through the glass. The doors were opened. She looked at the roll of burgundy carpet spread out before her, ending at the gutter.

The car door was opened. She stepped inside.

'Nobody is,' she whispered as the car sped away.

CHAPTER EIGHT

THE WAITING ROOM at the clinic was light and bright and cheerful. Magazines lay neatly stacked in a wall rack and a water cooler offered its shimmery blue contents silently beneath.

Above the sofa opposite a screen flashed news from an announcer as a tape of stories ran underneath. To her left the white-uniformed staff competently filed and welcomed and attended to various other things.

Ruby sat alone. Upright and alone. Her knees were locked together and she gripped the edge of the chair—waiting.

She glanced up at the staff, wondering when she would hear her name. And then she did. And she jumped so suddenly people turned to stare.

A uniformed, clean-faced woman holding a clipboard raised her eyebrows. 'Nobody with you?'

Ruby shook her head. When would people stop asking her that?

The woman softened slightly, cast a glance over her. 'Follow me.'

Ruby placed her weight carefully on her feet and stood. There was no pain. It was fine. It was all going to be fine. She followed the woman through a set of doors. A long corridor stretched ahead. She'd never been in this hospital before. The medical team normally came to the studio. But her physician had a clinic here and had specifically told her to come to the hospital for her final meeting.

Since she'd learned that her mind had run and her stomach had lurched. This incessant scrolling through every spinal, disc and musculature injury had got out of control. It didn't necessarily mean it was bad news, just because she wanted to see her here. Maybe she preferred to do her consulting here. Maybe all sorts of things might explain the gnawing aches, the awareness she had that she didn't want to listen. Maybe it would all be nothing.

But she had been through all the maybes in her head. It wasn't going to be good news. No one else had been asked to come here. She could only hope it wasn't really bad news.

'Come in, come in,' the consultant said, standing up when she opened the door, then nodding to the nurse. 'Have you brought anyone with you?'

Ruby stifled the urge to snap at her and shook her head instead.

The room was a square sterile box, with a window at the back and a desk facing the wall. She stared closely at the paper files on the desk, at the slice of computer screen she could see angled away to one side. She sat down on the chair she was offered—carefully. There was no twinge of pain. She was going to be given the all-clear. She could go back to rehearsals. It was going to be OK...

'Your knee,' said the doctor. 'How has it been?'

'Since the brace came off—nothing. I've been incredibly careful. All the physio and hydrotherapy—that's made a difference. My diet—I've followed every instruction. I can't wait to get back.'

'And the other pain?'

'It's almost gone, I think. I barely notice it.'

The doctor nodded. 'We did some blood tests, as you know, after you mentioned this new pain in your back.'

She knew. She'd been feeling so tired, so lethargic. She pressed her knees together and sat up as straight as she could. She angled her chin and stared ahead, ready to hear the next words. She'd heard those kind of words before—that was all they were. Words. There was always hope after the shock.

'Is there anything you want to tell me?'

The consultant had turned to read the screen, scrolling through the notes.

'No? In that case, I should tell you we screened for pregnancy as well as other things. I don't know if you're aware of that?'

A hammer fell in her head. Why was she saying that word? *Pregnant.* What did that have to do with anything?

'It's routine in medicine. With women of child-bearing age it's always a consideration.'

That hammer fell again as another thought forced its way through. The tiny voice that had been talking to her, whispering it.

Pregnant.

She'd refused to hear it, had blocked it out.

The hammer crashed the barrier down and suddenly she could see what she had known was there—the hideous thought that had been lurking in the shadows of her mind.

The whole world spun into a sickening swirl as a wave of nausea from low in her tummy rose up.

'I think that would explain all your other symptoms too. You know—the low blood pressure. That can happen. And back pain can be a symptom for some women. I wasn't sure if you already knew.'

'But I'm a *dancer*.' She looked into the pleasant face of the other woman.

'Dancers have babies,' she said, as if that was the most obvious and delightful thing in the world.

'But I *can't* have a baby.'

'Is there a reason why not?'

Her mother's face swam into view—frowning, angry, tearstained. Ruby was sitting beside her on a park bench as a little girl, putting her hand on her mother's leg to comfort her—she had long, slim legs, like hers. She jerked away, stood up.

'Are you OK, Mummy?'

'No, Ruby—I'm not. I'm not OK. I hate this life!
It's so unfair...'

She'd never said what fair would be, but Ruby
knew it wasn't this. She'd never smiled when it was
just them. But she'd been happy when someone else
was there—she would light up, laugh and sparkle.
And then she would like it when Ruby would dance.

'Come and dance for us, Ruby.'

They'd all smile and everyone would be happy,
and the coldness and fear would slide away because
Mummy *liked* it that she could do this for them.
Mummy loved her then.

And that was all she'd wanted—to see her
mother smile, to make her happy. But the music
would end, the people would go, and they'd be left
alone again. That aching, empty sadness would fall
around them.

She'd lie in her bedroom, listening to the sounds
of her mother, knowing that Mummy wanted to be
out with her friends, praying that she wouldn't leave
her alone again. The house was so dark, so quiet, so
empty... She'd hear her own heart beating, hear the
fear creeping through her, hear every single sound
in the house.

The ping of the kettle was good, and the striking
of a match to light a candle, the lights being turned
off and Mummy's feet on the stairs. But sometimes
she'd hear other sounds—the slide of the cupboard
door, the rustle of a raincoat, the drag of keys along

the shelf, the pause, the whoosh of the world outside, the silent click…

No, she couldn't have a baby because she couldn't have that world again. She couldn't look after a baby and give it everything it needed. She couldn't cause that pain. She could only keep her own pain at bay by dancing and rehearsing over and over and over. She couldn't be responsible for another living soul.

'I understand it's a shock. There's help available… I wasn't sure if you knew already. I can arrange for someone from the ballet company to speak to you— your mentor? Or there are services here. Is there no one close at hand? The father?'

The father. Matteo Rossini. What on earth had she been thinking? His face. His smile. His body. His never-ending stream of women.

This is what happens when feelings are given space. This disaster!

He was the worst possible person she could have let her guard down with. The very worst. She'd thought he might, just *might* get in touch with her— but, no. There had been nothing. He'd have had another whole troupe of women in his bed since then.

Would he even acknowledge that this had happened? He had been extremely careful with contraception. She had been reassured when he'd taken care of it so well because she knew she couldn't afford to get pregnant. She couldn't be a mother…

She put her hand out into the space that swam around her. Seconds, days, years suddenly spun ahead of her, showing her a different world that she could never in her worst nightmare have imagined would be hers.

'Let me get you some leaflets. We can talk about options.'

She couldn't talk about options. There *were* no options. He would have to take responsibility and let her get on with her life. There was only that. She couldn't mother anyone. She couldn't and wouldn't do that.

She breathed in, filling her lungs with air, willing her legs to be still, praying for the strength to stay calm and cope. Focus.

She stood up. 'So, just to be clear,' she said slowly. 'I am ready to go back to work. The ligaments are fully repaired and I won't be risking doing any damage. You're sure of that?'

'Your body will start to change during pregnancy, but you'll get all the help and advice you need.'

Her body would change? Her body was her only weapon in this world. She needed it to work.

Her throat closed over a new wave of fear.

Focus. Focus, she told herself, refusing to let it wash her away. *You've come so far. You're nearly there. It's just like those early calls to Mum. Focus on the good parts—ignore the rest or it'll pull you down.*

She swallowed again. 'My blood tests were clear? I'm in perfect health?'

'Ruby, you're pregnant. I can see that this is quite a shock and I'm here to help and advise.'

She lifted her bag onto her shoulder, looked inside it—her purse, her phone, her keys. One, two, three—all there. Everything was there. Time to go. She checked her watch. Eleven-thirty. An empty day ahead. But soon her days would be full again.

One step at a time.

'Thanks. I'll let you know if I need anything. What a beautiful day,' she said staring past the doctor's head to the trees and the sky outside.

She retraced her steps along the corridor, past the nurses' station, where their chatter was bright and chirpy, past the television and the blue water cooler, past the automatic doors and out into the warm sunny morning.

She could go back to rehearsals now. That was amazing—the hugest relief.

You're going to have a baby.

She should call someone to tell them the news. That she was able to dance. She should call someone and not think of anything else. Her mind whirred. Her heart pirouetted in her chest. They were about to start rehearsals for the winter season. She had a good chance of getting a principal role.

December.

Her heart sank. What size would she be? There was no chance of her being cast in any role, in any performance. There wouldn't be any point until after the baby was born.

And what was she going to do until then? More coaching and more watching? And then—childcare?

She could never afford that. Not on her salary, in London, alone.

Her feet were moving—left, right, left, right. She was at the underground station. She went down the steps. People thronged past her. She walked to the platform, felt the unbearable heat surround her. The noise of a train rumbled in the distance. People flicked their eyes at the information screens, fanned their faces in the stifling heat.

Like a dragon roaring closer and closer, the train finally loomed into view, lights like eyes blasting through the trapped turgid air.

There really was only one thing she could do.

CHAPTER NINE

MATTEO FASTENED THE cuffs of his shirt. He buttoned the single button on his suit jacket and straightened his collar. Tie or no tie? No tie. And no pocket square either.

He checked his image in the mirror one last time. It wasn't great. His hair needed a cut, but he hadn't had time, and he'd nicked his cheek shaving.

At least his lack of sleep was hidden under a mid-summer Mediterranean tan. And it had been worth those two days on a yacht, convincing some of the wealthiest men in Europe to become part of the bank's youth sponsorship programme. That had felt good. And it didn't do any harm that it would *look* good—this was a week when appearances mattered.

He walked to the dressing table, collected his keys and phone. He pressed the screen, opened the contacts, scrolled until he found the one he wanted: *Ruby, Ballet*. It was time he deleted that number. He'd been right not to chase her—she was too much trouble. He'd barely been able to concentrate since that night, and there was no time or space for that right now. He'd had a lucky escape, truth be told.

He tugged his cuffs down one last time and walked through the immense French doors to the grand terrace of the Château de la Croix.

David had done a brilliant job. He'd really pushed the boat out arranging the Cordon d'Or Regatta this year, leasing this fabulous former home to royalty and movie stars from days gone by. There was nowhere finer than the Bastion St-Jaume, and no better event in the entire social calendar of the Riviera. Tonight the high-rollers and big spenders would descend. And the die would be cast.

Outside the finishing touches were being set. Three huge marquees dotted the immaculate lawns that ran down from the swimming pool through densely planted palms and onto the beach beyond. Already the château's tiny harbour was filling up with launches as people journeyed in from ships anchored further off shore. Above, the sound of rotors slicing the air announced the arrival of the media, here to set up camp to get the very best shots of the A-list as they arrived.

And among them would be the sedate and conservative, deeply pious Augusto Arturo and his wife Marie-Isabelle.

Matteo walked through the sea of white-linen-covered chairs and cotton-draped tables to where the local media were setting up their shots. Huge gold ribbons encased each area, along with banners of golden silk. Bouquets of white roses were draped artistically across the tables and around the arches. Under one of these, the first guests to arrive had gathered—the kids who had sailed in the Medaille d'Argent that morning and were already toasting their own bravado.

He envied them their carefree youth. He'd been that naïve once, imagining his life could be built on his passions instead of being the pure, hard slog it had become.

'Looks like it's shaping up, David,' he said as he took a beer from his assistant and turned to walk with him. 'Everything going to plan?'

'So far so good. Arturo and Marie-Isabelle will arrive in half an hour. I'll hold back all the other guests until they're safely inside. Couple of pictures and then you can take them onto the west terrace. The sunset will be beautiful. You'll be irresistible, I'm sure.'

'And Claudio?' he said. 'Do you think he'll try and pull off any more dirty tricks?'

'Well, the montage of your exes on *The Finance Report* last night wasn't exactly helpful, but what else has he got?'

Matteo paused. What else *did* he have? Someone was drip-feeding the media with stories of his former girlfriends, trying to raise questions about his ability to lead the bank, never mind his morality.

'Nothing that I'm aware of, but that doesn't mean he won't try. He might claim he's got bigger fish to fry and we still need to cover every angle. I don't want a single drop of his poison to land on this.'

'I've analysed it from every single angle and back again. I can't see anything coming at you now that we're not prepared for. We've lived through Fayegate, after all. Could it get any worse? Nothing came of those pictures of you with that dancer at the ballet premiere, despite how they tried to paint it.'

'That's true,' he said.

They'd reached the edge of the lake. Matteo stared across the dark green water, his mind filling with images of a beautiful woman with fear in her eyes.

He thought he knew women, but that morning he'd come to realise he knew nothing. He'd been all set to make a commitment as far as a second date, when—*bam!*

'You're not my type.'

He might not know women, but he knew a lie when he heard one.

He shook his head, shook her image out of his mind, and turned to look back up at the château. It was already aflame with stars of the media and finance, locals and internationals. People came here to have a really good time and then go on to have an even better time somewhere else.

Well, not he. He had traded in those chips. That night with Ruby had unsettled something in him and he hadn't chased anything since, no matter how hard his friends had pressed him.

He pulled out his phone, checked the time—less

than ten minutes until curtain-up. Time to get back in the zone.

It was all hanging on him tonight. His mother had pulled back even further from the daily grind of the bank. It was as if the closer he got the further away she went. But it was good that she was feeling fulfilled, working with her kids in Africa. He'd never heard her happier since Dad died.

God, he missed him. He missed him so much.

He touched his wrist with his right hand, wrapped his fingers around his father's watch—the one thing that had survived the crash. He ran his thumb over the ridges of the dial, feeling the imprint of every etched line, remembering the times he'd cursed that watch because it had survived, ticking on while his father perished.

They would never be able to prove that Claudio had caused the accident. No one could accuse him of opening that bottle of whisky and pouring it down his father's throat. But he was the one man who had known about his alcoholism—the one man who'd been there with him when he'd battled it and won.

He'd been the man to drive him back there, too. He and his father had had a fight and the next thing they'd known he'd stolen his clients, started his own bank and then walked back into their lives goading them and gloating over his victory.

The day of the funeral—that fateful day—things had risen to the surface like so much toxic oil. Claudio had walked towards him, arms outstretched. All the signs of *Let's bury the hatchet for your father's sake*. And Matteo's urge to be comforted, reassured, had been huge. Here was his father's best friend, full of remorse, come to console him. He'd wanted it so badly. Despite everything he knew about Claudio he'd wanted to keep something of his father alive— even a corrupted friendship.

He'd been ready to forgive until, deep in Claudio's embrace, he'd heard those words.

'Get your hands off my son.'

And he had seen his mother, white-faced, grief-stricken, standing alone behind him.

'Don't you touch him. Don't you dare come here to start your tricks again...'

And then he had known. The suspicion that had wormed black holes into his brain had taken hold and a sickening rage had fallen. It was his *father* Claudio had loved—not his mother. That was the reason for his presence that had shadowed their lives for years.

His father—his hero, his rock.

Who was the man they'd just buried?

Ashes and dust and the truth gone with him. And Matteo's own world had crumbled and died too.

His paralysis had been broken. He'd lunged forward and bone had met flesh. His mother had screamed. Vases full of flowers had crashed to the ground. Women had shrieked and men had jumped forward. Hands had heaved at him, pulling him back as he'd struggled to get his hands on him. But Claudio had stepped away, clutching his jaw, spitting through the blood.

'*Get out of here! Get out of our house or I'll kill you!*'

He remembered his own roar. He remembered the words. He remembered the faces of the police officers as they told him they weren't going to charge him for assault but that he was lucky. And that he'd better give up on the idea of blaming anyone for his father's death. There was no way he could prove that the alcohol in his bloodstream was the responsibility of anyone but himself.

His mother had been inconsolable, sobbing. Words she'd never dreamed she'd say had finally tumbled out, confessing her secrets while he'd held her grief-wracked body close.

He learned that his father's relationship with Claudio had gone further than friendship.

They'd battled it together. She'd stood by him once, but she would not do it a second time.

And then that journey back to St Andrew's. The urge, the yearning, the need to see Sophie, to see her smile and feel her arms and let himself go, let it all out. But he hadn't been able to do that, because she had stood there naked, with another man. Betrayal had been everywhere he looked. Nothing had been safe, nothing sure. Love was worthless.

'Matteo?'

David's voice.

'Hmm…?'

'Maybe you should head up and start hosting. Things seem to be hotting up already.'

He was here. It was now. His father had done what he had done. He was never coming back, but after years of work the bank might just make it back to where it had once been. He might just pull this off. He might just be able to feel as if Claudio's dark shadow wasn't going to hang over them for ever.

He stared at the crowd of youngsters who'd now dispersed and were wandering through the rose bushes at the edge of the steps, with a photographer snapping them here and there as they moved.

'Let's go,' he said.

He strode up the lawn. People turned to stare. He could feel the interested glances of women and their light-voiced laughter like torches lighting his way up the path.

White marble steps appeared. He bounded up them. At the top were more of the young men and women who'd won the Medaille d'Or that afternoon. Bronzed and happy and on their way to a good time. He shook hands and kissed cheeks, walked on through the throng.

Faces swam before him—bright, smiling faces, so much happiness. The bank's brand was really on the rise. It was just what his father would have wanted. They were finally back in the big league.

He took all the praise with a smile, but it still felt undeserved. Until they had those extra clients from Arturo Finance he wouldn't feel back in the black.

He walked across the terrace, putting his empty water glass on a tray and stretching out his hand to shake that of the man coming towards his—the town's mayor, with his wife.

Wasn't it a marvellous event this year? So exciting!

He introduced the mayor to the winning team, photographs were taken, and they shuffled indoors as the next guests arrived. An actress and her boyfriend, fresh from Cannes.

She was looking as exquisite as ever! Was she showing at Cannes?

He listened to her reply as they too swung round for pictures. Over her shoulder David signalled Augusto and Marie-Isabelle's arrival.

Matteo felt grim determination clutch at his heart. There was no reason to feel anxious about this and every reason to feel confident. All the signs were there—this was the delicate first step in talks towards a merger. Arturo wouldn't have come if they weren't going forward. But it was the old-fashioned way. Private talks to build the relationship, get the chemistry right, and only then would the lawyers be given clearance to tidy up the deal.

He watched Augusto Arturo exit the car, saw the care the old man took over his wife, waiting while she adjusted her dress, offering her his arm as they looked up and smiled and began the slow climb to meet him.

And then, out of the corner of his eye, he saw the flash of something red—something that was burned deep on his subconscious. His heart thundered. His groin tightened.

He turned back to see Augusto and Marie-Isabelle, heads down, still climbing up. He swung his head to the left to see David. His assistant's face had changed from looking composed to a full-blown frown. He saw cameras begin to flash and felt a wave of interest pass over him and the others on the steps in the direction of the figure in red.

He turned now—fully stared. And there between two security guys, eyes fixed, wearing the same cherry-red, wide skirted dress, was... *Ruby?*

He stalled for a second, framed by guests and cameras, on the cusp of the most important moment of his business life. His heart crashed into his throat. Not another woman come to make a scene? Not now. Surely...?

But there was no mistaking it was her, and in a split second he read the situation. The two security were doing their, job checking to see if she was welcome or not, but they stood back respectfully, awed by her bone-deep beauty, her consummate elegance, her spirited challenge.

As if the rest of the world had dissolved he saw her she looking at him steadily, imploringly, with some deep, dark message, and he knew something was up. Something really big.

In a second David was at his side. 'You want me to take care of this?' he whispered as he slipped behind his shoulder.

Matteo's hand automatically reached for David's arm, holding him in check.

Augusto's sharp eyes watched everything even as he held out his arm for his wife, who was mounting the last step. Matteo glanced back at Ruby, then to Augusto, who now approached with his wife on his arm.

They were only a metre apart.

This was his moment. The tone, the chemistry of their welcome had to be right. He had to pull this off without a hitch or everything else would fall like a house of cards.

Around him people sensed the tension and began to crowd closer. David hovered expectantly.

Whatever she wanted, she would have to wait until they were safely settled away from cameras.

He stepped towards the couple, arms outstretched. 'How lovely to see you both. I'm so glad you could come.'

From the corner of his eye he saw the solitary red figure step closer.

'Can I speak to you, Matteo, please?' she said, her voice as clear as a midnight bell.

For a second he froze. The world was here—watching, waiting. He was swimming in a sea of staring faces with only one lifeline.

'*Darling* Ruby. You're *here*!' he said, hating himself. But he would not drown—not now.

They all turned to look at her. Marie-Isabelle was happily curious, but Augusto was no fool. Matteo's heart thundered faster. David's eyebrows shot up. And Ruby stood there, her dark eyes burning with a story he didn't yet know and couldn't risk hearing in front of this man.

Because she could ruin him. With a single phrase she could lay months of work to waste, destroyed. Another untrustworthy woman…another disaster ahead.

He kissed Marie-Isabelle's powdery cheek and dipped his head respectfully. 'If you'll excuse me for a moment. David will take you straight through to the terrace. I shouldn't be long.'

He turned just as Augusto's shrill voice cut in. 'Please invite your lady-friend to join us. The lovely young lady in red. Isn't she the dancer you were photographed with in London last month? We saw the feature in the press. I would be *delighted* to meet her. Wouldn't you, my dear?'

Marie-Isabelle smiled graciously.

'What a lovely idea,' said Matteo, and with a slight nod he took two paces across the carpet, past the curious faces, and lifted Ruby's hand into his.

He didn't pause to look at her or at anyone else as they moved off together, as if to the music of some practised *pas de deux*.

Away from the guests, down a short flight of steps and through some huge French windows, he led her into a drawing room full of nothing other than heavy antique furniture and vast windows that lent no privacy.

'Whatever you've come to say, you'll do so in private,' he said, moving briskly through the hallway, scanning the area for signs of listening ears or probing cameras.

'That depends,' she said.

Her fingers were snug in his hand. He felt a certain satisfaction from that, even as her words put him on guard.

'How did you know I was here?' he said as they breezed through the house and up the wide staircase.

Staff bustled about everywhere. Rooms all over the house were being used to interview the various stars who were due to arrive.

'You're not exactly hard to find,' she said, and he tried to hear in her voice the emotion that had caused her to come. There was an edge, a steely forceful tone through her words that put every nerve in his body on guard.

'Of course,' he said, thinking that she, too, would have seen the photographs of them at the benefit.

He wondered if she'd felt any of the yearning he'd felt as he'd scanned the press coverage of that night. Discretion hadn't been top of their list, he'd realised.

'You'll have seen, then, that this is the biggest Regatta we've ever attempted. And my mother's still in Africa so it's just me this year—and the biggest A-list donors we could find.'

As well as the start of talks with Arturo. Did she know she was exposing him to gossip just by being here?

The stress hormones in his blood were pumping higher and higher as he hurried them along silken rugs, down a high-ceilinged corridor flooded with light from an immense circular window at the end, right above the terrace where—please, God—David was keeping Augusto and his wife quietly entertained.

'In here.'

He opened a door on the left and led them into a bedroom, then paced around opening doors into cupboards and an en-suite bathroom. With microphones and lip-readers everywhere you couldn't ever be too sure, but it seemed safe.

He walked back across to where she stood—a vision in red that he would never forget.

'How is your knee?'

She closed her eyes, and the sweep of those eyelashes tugged at the memory of that night, that beautiful night…

She nodded. 'Fine. All clear. I'm back dancing full-time. For now.'

'Good…that's good.' He nodded.

For a second a smile lit her up, then vanished into the sorrowful beautiful hollows of her face.

'You look well. You suit this dress very much.'

'It's the only one I have. I thought I'd better make an effort or they might not let me gatecrash your party.'

'There was no need for you to gatecrash anything. You could have said—'

'I'm pregnant,' she blurted.

'You're what?' he said.

An instant image sprang into his mind—Ruby, plump with child. Her figure full and soft and feminine, rounded and abundant with life.

But not his—surely not his? It *couldn't* be his. But she was here. She'd tracked him all the way to France…

'It's yours.'

The words he most dreaded punched him in the stomach like two fists.

'No…' He started shaking his head. 'You can't be. It can't be— Are you sure? *Pregnant?*'

He sank down into a chair. His hands were in his hair, on his face, He stood up, staggered around. She stood staring at the space he'd been in, her own face a complete mask, showing nothing.

He strode over to her. 'How can you be? Didn't we…? Weren't you…? When did you find out? Oh, God…'

He paced again—to the bathroom. He opened the door and turned on the tap, let cold water gather in his hands and splashed it on his face. He stared at himself in the mirror.

Pregnant? He was going to be a father. No, no, *no.*

A *father*? This wasn't the face of a father!

He wasn't cut out for that. He wasn't even cut out for his own path in life—he hadn't led the bank back to glory yet—never mind starting a family. He could never be a father—not now, like this.

He walked back out. She was still there, standing exactly as he'd left her.

Her shoulders were straight, a delicate blend of bone and muscle and satin skin. Her slim arms were folded at her waist. Her wrists lay crossed over her tiny stomach. Her chin was high and proud. This woman he had spent one single night with was now bound to him for life. The path of his life had just taken another unforeseen fork.

Dear God—what had he done?

He thought of the château, the guests, the Arturos waiting. He thought of his mother's face, his father's smile, the mess he'd made of his life, of his one chance to get the bank back to where it should be.

And he thought of this woman—this beautiful creature standing before him, creating a life with him.

What the hell had he been thinking? Why couldn't he have been more careful?

Augusto. He had to get downstairs, manage this, calm everything down and then salvage the situation. He had to steer the ship away from the rocks.

'Who have you told?' he asked. 'Does anyone else know? I need to know what I'm dealing with here. When will it hit the press?'

He reached for her, felt the perfection of her limbs, the warmth of her skin and the silken twist of her hair against him. But instantly she pulled away.

'The *press*?' she said, her voice strained and shrill. 'Is that all you can think about?'

'Of course not. But they're here. They'll have a field-day if this gets out.'

'It's going to get out sooner or later. And if you don't stand by your responsibilities—*that's* when you'll need to worry.'

'I'll stand by my...*responsibilities*. There's absolutely no question of that.'

But he had other responsibilities right now. He had to get back to the Arturos. He had to calm this down, give himself some thinking time and then come back to it.

'You're right—you will. I didn't do this by myself. I need guarantees that you're not going to disappear and leave me to bring this baby up alone.'

Panic laced her every syllable and as he stared at the fear in her eyes he realised she had been dealing with this for weeks, while he was still running to catch up with the news. But the fact that she'd come here to tell him in person, choosing a moment when she knew he was under the spotlight, worried him. He had to keep this under control or he would lose his mind, and everything else with it, right in front of the world's press.

'Hang on. One step at a time. I'm still getting my head around it. I've got the deal of the century on hold down there and you think you can drop a bomb-shell like this and it's all OK?'

'*OK?* I don't think *any* of this is OK. I was just getting back to work—this is a complete disaster for me. I can't train... I can't perform. I'll miss the winter season and then what happens after that? What do I do?'

She threw up her hands and looked around wildly.

Matteo spoke again. 'We need to sit down calmly and talk it through. But there's plenty of time for that...'

'I never wanted children. I never even wanted to sleep with you. And now I have to have a child with you. This is the worst possible thing that could have happened to me.'

'Ruby, I'm sorry,' he said, choosing his words as carefully as his pounding heart would allow. 'But that's not how it was. You absolutely did want to sleep with me. You can't pull that excuse now and turn this into something that I *made* you do, as if this is all my fault.'

Her face twisted wretchedly. 'I still can't believe it. I still can't believe my whole life is over because of one stupid mistake.'

A burst of pride flared up in him. He'd never heard a woman describe him as a 'mistake'. Since Sophie, he'd been damned sure to keep women where he could manage them. The only stupid mistakes happened when he didn't.

'Your life isn't over,' he said coldly. 'This is a child we're talking about here. *My* child. But there are people waiting downstairs for me. I still have a business to run and I really need to go and sort it out. I'll come back and discuss this with you afterwards. Like adults.'

'Don't patronise me. Don't you think I *know* we're talking about our child? But you'd rather go and discuss business—that says it all.'

His phone vibrated in his pocket. He stared at her. Almond eyes, blurred and wild. Outside the band struck up another tune...a wave of laughter rolled in through the open windows.

'I will stand by you,' he heard himself say. 'My family means the world to me, and if there's going to be another part of it then I will do the right thing. There is no question of that. But this isn't the only thing going on right now...'

The phone continued to vibrate. It could only be David. The Arturos... He pulled it out.

'It was the *west* terrace, Matteo...?'

'On my way.'

'I have to go down there,' he said, slipping his phone back in his pocket. 'I know this is the worst possible timing, but David will come up and make sure you're comfortable. We can work out the other arrangements as soon as this is over. Just give me some time.'

'Do I have any choice?'

'No.'

He couldn't look at her face, but those dark eyes burned all the way to his heart as he strode to the door and out into the hall. The sounds of the party rumbled up to meet him. There were people smiling, posing, cameras everywhere. He pushed back through them, some sort of smile fixed on his face, giving a white-knuckled handshake to the people who stopped him.

He made his way to the west terrace. There they were. Marie-Isabelle was sitting on an elegant wicker chair, with a glass of champagne and a beatific smile. Augusto stood over her, and both were staring out over the marina to where the dipping orange sun was sinking low on a slick indigo sea.

'Ah. You've found the marvellous sunset,' he said, hearing words that meant nothing dripping out of his mouth. 'The best night of the year so far, don't you think?'

'Indeed… A night to talk about love, not money,' said Augusto. 'Where is your young lady? You should be spending time with her, not sitting with a pair of old fogeys like us.'

Matteo looked at him sharply, guilt settling in his stomach like acid. Augusto couldn't possibly know that he'd left his 'young lady' abandoned upstairs with her terrible secret. He had to swallow it down and get on with the job in hand, even though he felt it was already slipping out of his grasp.

He'd just put the whole Lady Faye nonsense behind him and now along rolled the next situation to deal with. The heavy yoke of his life suddenly felt like iron around his shoulders. He couldn't take much more, and now there was a child on the way, and Claudio would be standing and watching, waiting for a single slip-up so that he could come over and trample what was left of his family into the dirt.

He looked around at the sparkling boats on the marina, at the couples wandering on the grass, at the dance floor pulsing with bodies, the terrace, the long sweep of the driveway where cars were still coming and going. People with nothing to worry about other than having a good time.

For a moment he saw only the cloudless skies of their liberty, and jealousy rumbled like thunder in his heart. He'd never asked for any of this. This bank… this life. He'd never been given a choice.

What if he were given a choice? What if he turned his back on his duty? What was the worst that could happen? The bank would be sold off. But money would still move about from London to New York to Geneva. Everyone would be all right. No one would die.

'The party is going very well. The youngsters who won the Medaille are in fine spirits, don't you think?' asked Augusto.

He swallowed, focused. The effort to answer was almost too much. Words were there, but dredging them to his mouth, saying them—what was the point?

He stared ahead.

So many people. His mother, abroad, relying on him. David—long-serving and loyal. All the employees of the bank. A whole endless stream of people who needed him to keep going. And now his baby— his child. And the woman who had lit a fire in him that he'd thought dead, and then left him cold in his bed before the sun had risen. The woman he was going to be tied to for years and years to come...

'Indeed. It looks like they're having the time of their lives.' Slowly he managed to whisper the words from his dry and dusty throat.

'You were a sportsman once—is that right?' Augusto asked, fixing him once again with his bright-eyed stare. 'There was talk of you going professional. You weren't always going to follow your father into banking?'

Matteo frowned. How did he know that? He must have done his homework. The old fox was as wily as his reputation. This was an interview, right enough. The game was still on.

'I was a rugby player. But it's been a long time since I played.'

'But you are quite sure that it's banking that is your passion now? Your world? You cannot lead well in any field without feeling passion. Otherwise you'll only ever be a manager.'

From the corner of his eye Matteo looked at Augusto's crinkled skin, the liver spotted hands, the sharp, inquisitive eyes.

How did he know? How was this old man he barely knew able to say words that cut to the core of who he was? How could he see the gnawing worry that he just didn't care enough and that was why the bank had never fully recovered?

Matteo fixed his gaze to the bunting fluttering

in the evening breeze. He could not look round. He could not even speak. He couldn't trust himself.

Augusto spoke on. 'Because we both know that the person who takes my bank on will be more than that. I need someone who believes in what they do—not just someone who'd be going through the motions. I have no time for that.'

The moment was here. Matteo could feel it. Time was waiting, and from this moment all would slide along one path or another. He had been given the choice. It was up to him now to shake his head and walk away or step forward.

'With every breath in my body I want to make Rossini into the bank it should have been. And I am convinced that our two brands are unique in what we offer. What I want is to talk it over with you.'

The old man's penetrating stare was deep and long, and Matteo battled to keep his raging emotions under control as he gazed back. He would not lose yet. He readied himself to keep going—to say whatever it took to convince him to give him a chance.

Finally Augusto nodded. 'We'd like that too. Come to the Lake House. In a fortnight.'

The heaviest weight fell from his shoulders—so hard he almost slumped in relief.

'And bring your lovely young lady. It's important that we meet her too. My dear, I think we've spent enough time with the youngsters for one evening. Shall we?' said Augusto, lending his wife his arm.

'It will be our very great pleasure,' Matteo replied. 'I'll tell her straight away.'

'We're old-fashioned, though. You're not married yet, so please don't be assuming any privileges under my roof.'

Matteo smiled and shook the old man's hand as warmly as his chilled face and frozen heart would allow.

Marriage...

Pregnancy...

This whole situation was unravelling faster than he could ever have thought possible. Almost out of his grasp. Almost lost.

But not quite. Not yet. All he had to do was convince Ruby to play along.

He watched the Arturos settle into their car and drive away. Then he turned on his heel. He had business to get on with.

CHAPTER TEN

IT HAD TO BE DONE. There had been no other way. She'd tried to call—lifted the phone a hundred times. But she simply hadn't been able to get the words out of her mouth to say so much as his name to the elite-sounding voice that had answered at Banca Casa di Rossini.

What if he wouldn't take her call? What if he denied it? Men with money like him—they could do anything they wanted. He could lie to the police, get a restraining order on her—anything was possible. Her own father hadn't had two pennies to rub together and *he* had managed to disappear off the face of the earth, shirking his responsibilities, pretending she didn't even exist.

So, until she had made up her mind as to how to approach him, all she'd been able to do was stalk him in the virtual world.

It had become a routine since the day she'd walked out of the hospital. Who *was* this man who was going to father her child? She had no idea. She barely knew his name.

She had traded in her whole world—her career, her childhood dream about to come true—for one night with him. Just because he'd made her smile and laugh, and kissed her and made her body come alive, made her want to do things she'd never wanted to do before, made her want to lie beside him long after she should have slipped out and away,

She had no doubt that was when it had happened—in the depths of sleep, when they'd found one another in their dreams and the fire had burned and engulfed them.

Making a baby was as easy as that. And two lives were changed for ever.

The horror of it clutched at her heart every time she opened her eyes. In the mornings she'd lie awake in bed, waiting for the hideous nightmare to creep over her again like a dead woman's shroud. Her career was over. She couldn't dance for the best part of a year. And, despite all her best efforts, her money was dwindling away.

Memories of the days before her mother had met George would rise like ghouls from the depths of her mind. Wintry mornings in their freezing council flat, painting pictures on the damp windows between the mould-mottled frames, longing for breakfast before school but too afraid to ask her mum in case it made her cry or shout or—worst of all—storm off and leave her.

That fatherless world. The shame of school, where everyone else had pictures to draw and stories to tell of dads who taught them how to swim and ride a bike. Where playground voices had risen in competition: *'My dad says...' 'My dad does...'*

She had known nothing about him. He had been just a man who *'lives far away and can't come back'*. Ignorance had been bliss—until the dreadful night she'd overheard her mother's slurred voice telling someone how *'Everything was fine until Ruby came along. If it wasn't for that kid I'd be in a different world right now.'*

She'd stopped asking about her father after that, and tried to bury the sickeningly shameful secret that she'd driven him away. Then she had found dance and her mother had found George and it had been as if she'd lost her mother too.

The only thing she'd had in her world was her body and the music and the steps and the shapes and the struggle to be perfect. If she hadn't found dance she'd never have made it this far.

Dance had given her confidence. And hope. And finally an understanding that a baby wasn't responsible for anyone's actions.

But now she had done *this*. She had turned off her own life supply and turned on another. This new life.

She would lie in the watery morning light, put her hand on her stomach—still flat and hard with muscle— and wonder what lay beneath. What little life was in there, burrowed away, safe until it was ready to be born?

How was she ever going to give it what it needed? What chance did she have of being a proper mother when her own life hadn't begun until she'd become a boarder at the British Ballet? They were her only family. And now she'd let them down too...

That thought would make her heave herself out of bed before she was sick. She'd clean up, then lie on the cold floor between her tiny bathroom and tiny kitchen and torture herself with fear. What if she was left alone with this? What if Matteo had already met someone else? What if he refused to see her? What if he denied that he'd ever met her?

A phone call to her mother had proved once and for all that being left alone was a very real possibility— because relying on her for help wasn't an option. Oh, yes, she'd said she'd come to London when the baby was born, but as Ruby had ended the call, and felt the sorrowful finality of her whispered 'goodbye', she had known that *See you soon* was the last thing in the world that would actually happen.

No, there had been no other way. She'd had to try and see Matteo face to face as soon as she could.

So she had followed him on social media and in the press until she knew almost everything about him—including the fabulous annual Cordon D'Or, which ten weeks after she'd left the clinic, was exactly where he was going to be this weekend.

It was perfect. She still had her Banca Casa di Rossini ID badge and she still had the dress she'd thought she'd never wear again.

With the hugest reluctance she'd dragged it out from the bag at the bottom of her wardrobe and had it cleaned and altered. A few centimetres at the waist was all she'd needed to allow the zip to close. She'd bought her first ever strapless bra, put on her make-up, and then, with no luggage other than her pass-port and her handbag, her stomach heaving with hormones and nerves, she'd climbed aboard a bud-get airline flight to Nice.

With cameras everywhere, there would be no bet-ter place to do it. He couldn't say or do anything bad to her with the world watching. She'd jumped in a taxi, pulled up to the château gates, flashed the badge and made her way through the crowds, over the lawns, and up the marble steps to where the rich and the talented had been kissing their hellos.

Her heart had lurched at the sight of him. The same tall, broad frame, the wide, sure stance. His hair had flopped over his brow and his head had been down like a panther about to pounce. He wore a dark suit and pale blue shirt, open at the neck. And, damn him, he'd looked even more handsome than she remembered.

She'd walked along the path, never taking her eyes off him, fully intending to blurt it out, right there on the steps, but as he'd turned and seen her, and shock had filled his eyes, something had held her back. Something in that look had held her in place, told her not to say the words yet. Some desperate warning that, miraculously, she had decided to heed.

But it was all about a deal.

As soon as he'd learned he was going to be a father he'd upped and left, gone back to his party. The deal was clearly more important than learning he was going to be a father. But what else had she really expected? And now she'd lost her chance to shame him in front of the world.

She walked to the window and stared down at the party.

The elderly couple were pulling away in their car. She saw Matteo raise a hand to wave them off and then he watched them go, standing still as the marble pillars on either side of him that held the roof aloft.

'That's your father,' she whispered to the baby growing silently within her. 'Your father that I barely know. I'm sorry…so sorry, my angel. I never meant this to happen. But whatever is best for you I will do it. I will fight for you—and I will make sure he does not abandon you.'

As she stared down at the top of his head he suddenly turned and looked up at the window, as if he'd heard her words. She met his eyes, and again that arc of something deep and strong sprang between them. He turned around fully now, as one, two, three more seconds ticked by, his steady gaze so powerful that it made her want to reach for something to hold on to.

Then he bowed his head and was gone.

Her heart began to thunder and her legs began to move. She wasn't going to stay hidden away up here a moment longer. She was going to go down to the party and find him—before he got tangled up in some other business conversation, or some woman threw herself all over him and she slid even further down his list of priorities.

She would not disappear because it didn't suit him to have a child. *Never.*

She moved across the room, put her hand out to push the door—but it landed instead on the wide, warm chest of Matteo.

Without missing a beat, he put his hand over hers and spun her around with him.

'Now we can get out of here.'

Her feet barely touched the ground as he sped them along the hallway, now flooded with late-evening sun and the faint glow of just-lit lamps.

'David, I need a launch out to the boat. Set it up. Clothes, food... But above all else—privacy.'

He slipped his phone away and at the top of the stairs he turned. 'We'll use the servants' entrance.'

'For what? What's going on?'

His jaw was grim, his mouth pinched, but he looked at her with surprise in his eyes.

'You wanted to talk. So we talk—without anyone listening. Offshore. I don't want any distractions.'

His dark berry eyes gave nothing away, but she could feel the energy pulsing off him in waves. He was bullish. He was going to take this head-on—she could see that. He wasn't running away.

'Do you have anything with you? Anything you need back at your hotel?'

She shook her head. 'I wasn't planning on staying any longer than necessary. This is all I have.'

'Doesn't matter. If you think of something David will sort it. OK—you ready for this? Because you'd better get used to it.'

He put his arm around her shoulders and steered them both out. She didn't raise her head above the trail of steps and gravel paths, the perfect lawns and flowerbeds, all the way down to the tiny beach and jetty where a sleek white motorboat was waiting.

He jumped aboard and the little boat bobbed with his weight.

'Take your shoes off,' he said as he held out his arm to help her aboard.

She stared at the slippery jetty, at its ridged surface, and then at the inky water and the huge gap between solid land and the boat.

'Come on,' he said, 'before we attract a crowd.'

He stretched his hand out a little further but she faltered.

'I'm a bit nervous of water. I can't swim properly.' It was a fact she hated to say out loud, but a fact nonetheless.

'That's totally OK,' he said, and she noticed with relief the lack of censure in his voice. 'You'll be completely safe—just do what I tell you. Take your shoes off first. Heels are dangerous on boats. Throw them to me and then put your arms out. That's it,' he said as she followed his instructions.

His strong hands gripped her arms, then her waist,

and then, as she stared up into his face, she gingerly stepped into the boat. It moved slightly, but his body was like a rock and she found herself holding on to it with both arms, just for a moment, but long enough to feel an echo of that hunger.

He lifted a life jacket and helped her into it, his fingers swift and deft, face focused. Then he unfastened the rope and sat down, pulling her by the hand to sit beside him. The engine fired up and they began to nose their way through the bay between the other boats, berthed like huge chess pieces on a watery board.

Suddenly they reached clear water and picked up speed. As the boat bumped along on the waves and out to the sea, spray landed on her bare arms and face and the wind whipped at her hair. She looked at him but he stared stubbornly ahead, eyes fixed on the horizon.

'Where exactly are we going?' she asked, as they rounded the bay and a huge white yacht came into view.

He nodded. 'On that—where I'm pretty sure we won't be disturbed.'

They pulled alongside and waited as the water impatiently slapped the sides of the boat and her sensitive nose picked up the scent of salty ocean mingled with fuel. As the rope was pulled tight, men appeared from nowhere—all of them poised, it seemed, to help her on board.

'OK, I've got this,' barked Matteo, and they melted away. 'Ruby?'

She slid her hands into his as he helped her aboard with what seemed suddenly like something close to gentleness. Then they walked up through one deck into another and right into the prow of the ship, where tiny lights were draped around the wooden railings and a single table was set for dinner for two.

'Oh!' she gasped. 'Is this for us?'

Maids appeared with vases of white roses and domed silver platters.

'For you,' he said, pulling out her chair as if it was no big deal. 'And just one more thing...'

He reached out and pressed a button and the roof retracted, opening them up to the starry sky above. The ship's mast stretched high, and from the top fluttered a little flag. The distant sounds of the party rumbled behind them and all around a warming breeze stirred the trails of bunting that clung prettily to the ropes.

It was the most romantic scene she'd ever witnessed. She had been prepared for denial, a fight, maybe even a pay-off, but she hadn't been prepared for kindness or consideration or—*romance*?

Maybe it was Matteo's way of softening her up, lulling her into giving in to his will. She sat straight in her seat. She wasn't going to make any of this easy for him.

'OK. We're here now, and we've got a lot to talk about, but I suggest we take this slowly,' he said, easing his large frame into the seat opposite with the grace that, even now, she found irresistibly alluring.

'I don't want to rush into talking about things that are bigger than anything we've ever had to deal with before. We're going to take a little time to get to know one another again—you know, build up some trust. You OK with that?'

He poured water into her glass, his eyes concentrating only on that, his face registering nothing other than patience. But it wasn't patience that she wanted to see. She needed reassurance. She needed action.

'I'm OK with that as long as you understand that I'm not here for dinner and dancing. I'm here for one reason only and that's to discuss next steps.'

He put his glass down slowly. 'All right. If that's the way you want to play it I can't force you. All I'm saying is that we're asking a lot of each other if we don't take our time here. I never get into talks cold. It's a really dumb thing to do.'

'You think forcing small-talk is really going to make a difference to the outcome?'

'I wouldn't dream of forcing my small-talk on anyone. It's not that great. But I assume you'll want to eat and that you'll at least stay until morning. There's loads of space here, and you'll need to rest in…'

The steepled hands, the patient, soothing voice again.

Instantly her hackles rose.

'Please don't patronise me by saying *in your condition*. I've survived the past few weeks of this pregnancy being sick in toilets, without your help, so I think I'm well aware of what I do and don't need.'

The silence with which he met her sharp words sat heavy and still.

'I'm sorry to hear that,' he said finally. 'I should have realised. It's not just coming to terms with being pregnant that you've had to cope with. It's all the physical things too. I've got a lot to learn.'

She looked sharply at him. This was not what she had expected. At all.

'Don't worry—the physical things only relate to the woman. You're quite safe.'

'OK, Ruby,' he said, obviously swallowing down on a chuckle. 'I know that I'm not going to be the one who actually goes through the pregnancy. I was only trying to say that I want to be part of this with you, and to do that I need to find out more about it. That's all.'

'You want to be part of this?'

He was *saying* the right things. He was making eye contact and acting concerned. But still...

'Yes, but, as I said, tomorrow is time enough for us to talk about all that. Why don't you tuck in? You must be hungry. And I know how much you like to eat.'

She lifted the dome from her plate to reveal a platter of ice and lemon and six fat oysters glistening in their shells.

'I can't eat these,' she said, looking up at him. 'I can't drink wine or eat soft cheese or lots of other things. And cream makes me sick. And soy sauce. Anything like that.' She pushed the plate away.

Matteo threw down his napkin, stood up and

walked around the table. Startled, she tilted her head back to look at him.

'You see—this is just the sort of thing I mean. I need to know how to look after you.'

He put his large hands out and she slid hers into them. Like some stupid marionette, she allowed herself to be lifted to her feet. She could feel the heat from his body, sense the strength from his core, the sure, solid presence that she'd once buried herself in, guard down and heart wide open.

'Come on. Let me show you to your cabin and I'll get some food that you can eat sent in to you. Food that's not going to harm you or the baby.'

She could feel herself sinking towards him, the magnetic pull of his body offering and demanding in equal measure, natural as sunset and sunrise, just like the last time. But she couldn't afford that luxury again. She had to keep herself apart, head clear and mind sharp as a tack.

He was using her weakness against her—making her dependent. She shook her head, ready to argue, but the waves of tiredness were huge now. She'd been on the go for hours, hadn't slept well the night before, and stress and strain and emotion were all beginning to drag her under. She opened her mouth in a deep yawn.

'That's it,' he said. 'No arguments. I'm taking control here and you're going to bed.'

'I will not be ordered around,' she muttered stubbornly. 'I'll make my own decisions and…'

But she was engulfed in another yawn and the last of her energy evaporated.

'Make your own decisions in the morning. Make all the decisions you like. But right now I'm in charge. Let's go.'

He scooped her up, and just that—the sensation of his body around hers and his fierce directive—had her lost in the waves of her own fight. She caved, allowed him to hold her close, didn't fight the warm glove of his hand on her head. Didn't fight the steady beat of his heart on her cheek or the warm male scent of his chest. She didn't lift her head to check where he was going, or worry or wonder how she was going to get home.

She let herself melt.

When he opened the door of a cabin she saw subtle lights and soft fabrics in creams and pinks and lacquered wood. And she didn't resist.

He laid her down on the bed and she felt his hands peel down her zip and ease her out of her dress. And still she didn't struggle. She let it happen. She rolled over in her underwear, felt sheets pulled back, and then she was enveloped in the softest satin and her path into dreams stretched out ahead.

And she knew, as she drifted under, that she was here again, with Matteo, and that the hole in her armour was getting wider and wider.

CHAPTER ELEVEN

ON HIS EIGHTEENTH BIRTHDAY his father had given Matteo the fountain pen he now held in his hands. He ran his fingers along the onyx lacquer and tested the brass nib. The first time he'd used it was when he'd had to sign the lease for his flat at university. It had felt like a step into adulthood, symbolically marked by such a formal object. It was a lovely pen—now used for signing contracts and legal documents—but it wasn't what he needed right now.

He put the lid on it and tucked it away.

Right now he needed something much more current. Something with no trace of the past. Something he could use to write out his future. Because it was right there, in front of him, fast asleep on the bed.

He stretched out his legs and rolled his shoulders. The chair was comfortable enough for short people who wanted to take a load off their feet for a few minutes, but it was totally useless for a six-foot-three ex-rugby-player who'd been folded into it for the past five hours.

But where else would he be with all the chattering in his mind, the constant conversations he'd been having with himself since he'd closed the door on the Arturos, watched them roll off down the drive and then turned to see that vision in red at the window.

She had his mind—every corner of it.

He'd better get it back—and fast.

He opened his black notebook and took another fresh page. Lifted a sleek rollerball, made two lists. Things he was going to jettison and things he was going to adopt.

Booze. That had to go. Not because he had a problem with it, but because it was always there at the back of his mind that he might one day. His single Friday beer was his way of showing that he had it under control. But he'd still had too many nights on the tiles he'd regretted, and his father had seemed to have it all under control. Except he hadn't. And it'd killed him.

He looked at Ruby's face, soft in sleep. There was no way he was going to have anything around him that might do harm to her or their baby.

Next to go—gambling. That wasn't going to be hard. He couldn't care less if he never saw the inside of a casino again. But it was the boys he'd miss. He needed his friends. He needed the camaraderie, the bluster and fun.

And more than that he needed to feel that physical force, that competition. It was rugby he really needed—he still missed it every day. But this wasn't about him. This was about doing the right thing. This was the future, not the past.

Ruby moaned in her sleep and he sat up straight in the chair. She was dreaming, mumbling softly, and he leaned closer, watching. Her ebony hair was fanned out on the pillow, her bare arm as pale as the sheet it rested on. He saw the faint scar of a needle jab and a series of pale brown moles, but they weren't imperfections. All they did was made her look even more beautiful.

He had never felt such responsibility in his life.

He had to keep her safe, keep her healthy and keep her onside at all costs.

He went back to his list, made another column. Wrote down, in slow, bold strokes *Marriage*.

He stared at the word, at the letters and the shape they made. Even writing it made him feel that he'd aged ten years. It was a word of maturity, selflessness. It was weighted with responsibility and expectations. Those letters were both a mirror and a map—forcing him to see what a lightweight he'd been these past years. The playboy, playing fast and loose, the toast of all his friends because he would not let any woman tell him how to run his life.

Sophie's face flashed through his mind. The horror in her eyes through the steam of the shower. Those wounds had scarred him deeply, but it was time to acknowledge them and move on.

Sophie was ten years ago. Ruby was now.

And even though he didn't want marriage, could

he bear his child to be brought up hundreds of miles away? By another man. Because if he didn't marry Ruby, someone else would.

Beautiful Ruby.

He checked his watch. She'd been asleep six hours. She was bound to wake up soon.

He wrote down *Home*. The answer to that word was going to depend a lot on the answer to the one above it. He'd ask her to marry him, she'd say yes, and they'd live in—London? Was that the best place to bring up the *bambino*? If he didn't ask her to marry him, could they live together? Where would that be? Would that work out better?

If they didn't live together the baby would be brought up in two homes. He'd need to stay more in London, or she'd need to come to Rome. He'd buy her a house, or move her into one of his. And what about her career? Didn't ballet mean touring and travelling? What then?

His own parents had led largely separate lives, he realised. But whatever his father's demons had been they'd stayed together, married, all those years. For the sake of him? The bank? His mother had loved his father—he knew that much. She'd fought for him. But at the end of the day Claudio had won. Whatever way you looked at it, marriage was a fake but probably necessary institution.

He put his head in his hands, ran his palm over his brow, felt the steady motion of the boat and the lure of sleep. The lure of sleeping beside Ruby. The thought of having her in his bed again—he'd tried hard to put it out of his mind, but who was he kidding? He hardened in response.

God, his mind was rammed with this and he hadn't even started to put the Arturo merger into the mix.

'What time is it?'

He looked up. She was propped up on her elbows, hair flopping all over her face, her cheeks pink and plump with rest and her eyes blinking awake in the soft light of morning. She looked sweet and vulnerable and his heart swelled.

He looked away. 'About six. Here,' he said, ignoring the pain as he stretched his cramped legs. 'I got you some tea and toast.'

She looked at him, then at the tray that had been sitting beside her for the past ten minutes.

'OK…thanks.'

'It's to prevent your morning sickness. I've been reading up about it. Have something bland first thing and it settles your stomach. So they say.'

'You've been reading up about morning sickness?'

'And other things.'

'Is that right? Anything else you found out?'

She sat up properly now, and as she moved the sheet dropped down, revealing her nakedness.

'Your breasts. They'll be tender. And getting bigger.'

She glared at him. 'That's none of your business,' she said, but she didn't rush to cover herself and he didn't rush to shift his gaze.

'I'm just stating a fact,' he said, taking in her softness, shaded in the morning light, as his voice deepened to a growl even to his own ears. 'And they're really pretty.'

Nothing moved but the steady rock of the boat and the solid beat of his heart in his chest. But all around his body his senses sparked to life. The air became hot as desire bloomed between them. Her chest heaved and she looked utterly undone already, with messy tendrils of hair hanging loose above the rosy pink tips of her nipples which, before his very eyes, were tightening into hard little nubs.

He hesitated. All he wanted was to grab her into his arms and fasten his mouth on hers. He wanted to mould her curves in his hands and tug them both into another sexual adventure. She was all he'd been dreaming about for weeks and she was right here, as ripe and ready for him as he was for her.

Not yet, a voice told him. *Not yet. Take it easy. She's vulnerable, and look what happened the last time.*

He needed way more than sex now. He needed her here, by his side, working things out together. This family, this merger, this life.

She reached for the sheet, pulled it up to her chest. 'If you don't mind…?'

He stood. 'Of course. Join me on deck for breakfast when you're ready. The shower's in there. David's delivered a load of clothes—just take what you want.'

He lifted his notebook, the pen. Took two steps and opened the door.

'As soon as you're ready we can talk.'

CHAPTER TWELVE

'OVER HERE.'

Ruby stepped out onto the deck into a brilliant blue-washed day, where sky met sea in strips of azure and indigo and shards of sunlight beamed like lasers all around. They were in the middle of nowhere. Literally not a speck of land was anywhere to be seen.

She looked up to see Matteo. He too had showered and changed. A tight white T-shirt stretched over his broad chest and light blue jeans hung low on his hips. Her eyes dropped automatically to the waistline and the erotic trail of dark coarse hair that disappeared into his groin.

He leaned over the railing, beckoned for her to join him at a table laid with breakfast things.

'You look lovely,' he said, reaching for her hand and helping her climb to the top of the ladder onto the deck.

For a moment she felt lovely too. Stepping into silk underwear and trying on summer dresses had helped to quell her nausea and for ten glorious minutes she'd felt like a little girl at the dressing up box, lost in a froth of pretty clothes.

'How was the toast? Did it work? Could you eat some more?'

She climbed the short flight of steps to the next deck and there saw a table awash with fruit and yogurt and baskets of bread. Hunger battled nausea and won. She was starving, but she wasn't going to accept anything until they'd had a proper conversation.

'Where are we?'

'Boats have a habit of moving when you untie them.' He smiled. 'Just a little bit of privacy, Ruby. I wasn't going to hang around the Riviera to find myself the subject of any more gossip. This—' he held out his hands '—is private. There's too much at stake for me right now to have anything go wrong.'

So she was right. He was keeping this under wraps. Alarm bells started to ring.

'I'm not going to hide away, Matteo. You can't keep me on a boat for the next seven months.'

'I don't plan to hide you anywhere. But staying back there wasn't an option. You saw the press there last night—I don't want anyone crawling around in my private life and I'm sure you don't either.'

'My private life is an open book,' she said, as spiky hackles rose on her skin. 'I've got nothing to hide.'

'This isn't about hiding, Ruby,' he said calmly. 'It's about getting time together away from everything else. This is big. Huge. We need to get our heads around it.'

'It's quite simple. We're going to have a baby,' she said, hearing the shrill note in her voice and hating how desperate she sounded. But she *was* desperate. If he didn't play his part she was as lost at sea as if she'd fallen overboard.

He sighed. He smiled. He put his hands on her arms and pulled her towards the chair.

'Yes, we are. And from here on in we're going to be adult about this. What's the rush? We've got plenty of time to talk things through. And as soon as we're both ready we'll tell the world. Not before. I don't want this to overshadow anything. I've got other stuff on the go and I want some time. That's all. That's not unreasonable, is it?'

'I suppose not,' she said reluctantly, calming at the lull of his voice and the gentle slosh of the boat on the water.

There really was no rush, she told herself. He seemed to be accepting it. He hadn't denied it or accused her of sleeping around. He hadn't howled or beat his chest or simply disappeared. He'd sat by her bed through the night and he hadn't made a move on her.

She felt her shoulders slump and a slow breath ease out of her chest. The steady slap of water on the boat and the endless hazy day seemed to smooth her hackles, quiet her mind.

'Come on. Breakfast.'

The lure of glistening melon and hot rolls was too much, and she sat down and reached for some bread immediately.

He nodded, poured water. Didn't do anything else.

She watched him as she buttered bread and popped it in her mouth. He watched her back. A bowl of berries appeared before her, topped with fresh yogurt and seeds. It looked so good she gave in and tucked in greedily, flicking her eyes up to him between bites.

He sipped coffee.

'Aren't you going to have anything?' she said, as she popped another piece of fruit in her mouth and buttered another roll.

'I've eaten. And this is much more fun. It's like watching locusts.'

She made a face and looked around, still hungry. She helped herself to more yogurt, piling it high on her plate.

'It was like this the last time too,' he said.

'Last time?'

'At the Italian restaurant? Luigi's? Don't tell me you've forgotten our first date. It was an amazing night…'

She sipped water and sat back as his words hung between them. Wisps of memory fluttered up into her mind—the fun, the camaraderie, the intimacy—tugging her back into that warm embrace. And he, right there opposite her, looked as if he was sharing exactly the same thoughts.

'How do you think it happened?' he asked quietly.

'We took precautions.'

She steeled herself to look up into his face.

'Not every time. There was once…in the night… when we were both half asleep.'

He raised an eyebrow. 'Yes. But something certainly woke us up.'

She heard the slight tone of amusement in his voice and looked down at her plate.

'Come on, Ruby. There's no point in being coy about it. We had something special going on that night. And it feels to me as if that part of a relationship at least might work for us.'

She felt the tug of that night, in those hours before dawn, the warmth of his body, the pleasure of her own melting into his arms. Those hours when she'd lost her head and everything she'd ever stood for. It was as if she'd paused her life when she'd gone into that apartment—as if she'd thought some other life might be possible instead of the one she'd been striving for.

And being here with him now she could see how easy it would be to step into the honey-trap again, but this was far too important. She had to stay focused. He needed to understand that this was real. They were both in it for the long haul.

'Matteo, no.' She shook her head. 'This isn't about us.' She laughed at her own stupid phrase. 'What am I talking about? There *is* no us. There's only a baby without a family. And I need to know what we're going to do about it.'

She stared at his face for the optimistic signs that she wanted to see. Signs that he wasn't going anywhere…

'You're really in a hurry over this, aren't you? The baby's not even born yet. Don't you think you're getting ahead of things?'

'You said last night that you're going to accept your responsibilities,' she said. 'But what does that mean? I have a career. I can't perform when I'm pregnant, so I'm going to have work in the school, and then, when I'm fit again, I'll go back to dancing. But I can't do it alone.'

'You've had longer to think this through, Ruby. I don't even know what you've got in mind. You live in London. I live in Rome *and* London. We both travel a lot. How is this going to work?'

'Of course it can work. I want to get back to dancing as soon as I can. I can't afford childcare on my own—I assumed you'd want to employ a nanny, no?'

He frowned at that. 'How soon do you mean?'

'A few weeks after the birth. I don't see why not.'

'Weeks?'

Something in that judgemental tone made her antennae twirl even faster. She'd already had a lifetime of being judged. Everyone had an opinion.

'A few weeks after the birth?' he repeated. 'I can see you're not impressed with my question, but it's a perfectly reasonable thing to ask.'

'I'm not going to justify my decision to you or anyone else.'

He sat back in his chair, the only real sign that he was surprised. He touched his fingertips together and just that tiny movement caused the muscles in his arms to ripple and bulge. Arms that she'd trailed her lips all over, that had held her in the tightest embrace.

Arms that would cradle a tiny baby in a few months.

She could see it as clearly as if it had already happened—as if he really was lifting a crying infant to soothe and protect it. And she knew then that he was going to cherish it. He was going to be a real dad.

It was just a single second's realisation, but it was as intense and terrifying as standing on the edge of a cliff. Because she was terrified she wasn't going to be able to do the same. Her heart started thundering in her chest again. Her own childhood had been a disaster. She had a broken relationship with her mother, felt nothing for her half-siblings. She'd never wanted a baby—and now it was really happening.

'Ruby, we're not at that stage of decision yet. We're still at the stage of coming to terms with this. OK, *I* am still at the stage of coming to terms with it.'

He lifted his phone.

'I'm still fielding calls, trying to explain where I disappeared to last night. I have a bank to run that isn't nine to five and I have all this—this other stuff going on. My head is rammed, Ruby. I don't want to make any decisions until I've had a proper chance to think things through. Who knows how we'll both feel later on?'

As he spoke his phone vibrated on the table as if on cue. He glanced at it, sighed, put it down again and looked out past the deck, shaking his head slightly as if he couldn't quite believe the mess he found himself in.

Behind his head the long straight strips of sea and sky blended in a haze of blue. The creaking and whooshing sounds of the yacht's gentle bounce through the waves were all she could hear. She looked at him, and for the first time saw the exhaustion on his face. He had sat up with her all night, squashed into a chair, and even though now he was clean-shaven and showered his features were drained and drawn.

He had read up on pregnancy and morning sickness and brought her toast, and that was maybe one of the nicest things anyone had ever done for her. Because she didn't let anyone do *anything* for her.

He turned round to face her.

'I know you're looking at me, wondering what the hell I'm all about and if I'm going to stick around. All you've ever seen is the party side of me—at the ballet benefit and then last night. Or in the press. You're wondering what kind of guy I am who has this trail of women behind him and won't settle down. And I don't blame you for thinking like that. I'd be exactly the same.'

He leaned forward, his arms and shoulders and chest and everything about him telegraphing pure presence, pure strength. And she was right back there, in that Italian restaurant, gazing at him with a lust she'd never believed she could feel for anyone.

The way he'd absorbed everything she'd told him and worked the room, the way they'd worked together, spinning the web of desire around one another until all her armour had melted away.

At least he'd been straight down the line. Then and now.

'You think I'm some kind of a flake who's going to leave you high and dry with a baby to look after, all on your own, and you're in a panic that maybe I won't even pay my way and look after things. I get it.'

'Yes,' she said. 'I am.'

But how did she tell him the rest—that she was more afraid of *herself.* She didn't want to let anyone into her life, to need or be needed by anyone. The only thing she needed in her life was herself.

He reached his big broad hand across the table and took hers, wrapping his fingers around it. She tried to pull it back but he held on.

'I'm going to do the right thing. I know you've no reason to trust me, but I want to help. I'm not the guy you think you know.'

And I'm not who you think I am, she thought. *I'll be no good at this. I'll let us down...*

Everything he said made her feel worse inside. She could see that he meant every word—and she believed him, she really did. But he thought she was like other women, wanting a baby and a family and all those things.

When they were the very last things she wanted.

She looked around the boat, a sudden sense of

panic engulfing her like a blinding, heavy sea fog, even though it was the clearest, freshest day she could ever imagine.

'Ruby.'

She felt a tug on her hand.

'Ruby,' he said, tugging again and dragging her gaze around to him. 'Don't worry. I would never, ever leave you alone with this. That's not who I am. And we haven't spoken yet about your family—telling my mother, your mother. We can do that together, if it helps?'

'I've already told her,' she said woodenly. She poured some water into a glass, then pushed it away.

'And?'

She looked at him. 'And what?'

'Was she happy for you? Is she going to be around when the baby's born?'

She wiped her hand in the air as if she was swatting away his silly idea. 'Oh, you don't need to worry about that. She'll be caught up with her own stuff.'

'How do you two keep in touch? Does she come to London much? You said she lives in Cornwall, right?'

'We manage on the phone.'

She didn't need to look up to see the frown cross his eyes. She felt his judgement unfurl like a blow and kept her eyes on the horizon.

'Right... I see. I suppose it's quite a commitment for her to travel up, but we'll work around that—and you've met my mother, so you know she's not the average stay-at-home type, although she'll want to play her part. But, hey, there's plenty of time to work all that out too. More tea?'

She shook her head.

'She'll be all right about it, you think?' she said, an image of his mother coming into her mind. She wasn't the type of woman who'd let herself get into trouble. She was a super-powered, super-organised over-achiever whose every second seemed to be planned and executed with complete precision.

Coral Rossini was going to judge her too, and at best she would look like an idiot, at worst a scheming gold-digger.

This whole situation was getting worse and worse.

'Can we start to go back to shore now?' she asked, looking round. 'I have to get back.'

He stood up. The look on his face was something she couldn't quite read. Frustration?

'Sure,' he said. 'We'll stop at one of the little islands on the way. It'll only take an hour or so and they're so pretty. Seems a shame not to show you this part of the world while you're here.'

She opened her mouth to complain.

'No buts. You've come all this way. You're my guest and I want you to have a little fun before you go back.'

He walked around the table, his big frame and long legs somehow stepping gracefully between the chairs, until he was right beside her. She looked up, shielding her eyes from the sun until he stood directly in front of it, casting a shadow, close enough for her to see the creases in his T-shirt and the links in the strap of his watch.

'I'm not really in the mood for fun.'

He held out his hand. 'Come on, stop trying to punish me. I know you're mad at me—and yourself. But we had a good time. And now we need to manage the situation as best we can. We'll be fine.'

He pulled her to her feet. He encircled her in his arms. Held her close.

And she closed her eyes and let the sway of the boat and the heat of his body hold her still. Between them was the little life they had made, sleeping and growing, blissfully unaware, blissfully safe.

CHAPTER THIRTEEN

THE LAST TRACES of the Mistral whipped at the pines, sending green waves rolling across the tip of the island. Cicadas relentlessly announced themselves from bushes, and overhead the pealing calls of gulls carried tales of what they'd seen and warnings of what was still to come.

Matteo, sitting in a striped deckchair, put down his papers and raised his sunglasses for a moment, straining to see a yacht that was dropping anchor out in the bay. Tiny figures scuttled around, then one by one jumped into the dinghy that would take them ashore.

Ashore to this haven—the exclusive Ile-St-Agnes, ten square kilometres of verdant land, home only to teeming wildlife and the ultra-rich. Its single hotel, reached only by chartered yacht, was where Ruby had eventually agreed to come ashore, to have a little stroll and now to rest stretched out beside him, under a parasol on a fat-cushioned lounger.

It had been years since he'd been here—years

since the annual holidays he'd spent there in his early childhood. He glanced at the little pool where children splashed noisily, and at the few people lying on loungers around the edges. That had been his parents once, with Claudio and his 'girlfriends'. Drinking martinis and smoking cigarettes, laughing and having fun together—the glamorous couple and their glamorous friends, the toast of the Riviera in their day, intact in their little bubble of happiness, years before the whole thing fell apart.

A waiter walked across the scene with a silver tray. He stopped to serve wine to an older couple on the terrace, sedately dressed, enjoying their lunch. Below them, on the loungers, a movement caught his eye—two women, sleek in their Saint Tropez tans. They'd been discreetly staring over at him, and were now doing it indiscreetly. They sat up provocatively, flirting, topless.

He turned his face deliberately away and looked at Ruby, who was watching with undisguised disdain.

'Friends of yours…?' she said, her dark eyebrows shooting up.

She scowled, turned her back and began to ease the red chiffon wrap from her shoulders, revealing a modest bikini beneath. Her waist was slightly swollen with their growing baby and her slim limbs glowed beautifully pale, obviously unfamiliar with hot sunshine. His heart surged with pride as he watched her.

'…they certainly look as if they'd like to be.'

He smiled at her snippy comment, watching as she squirted a dollop of sun cream on her hand and began to smooth it down her arms. As she attempted to rub her back the twin blades of her shoulders flexed accusingly.

'Allow me,' he said, reaching round and lifting the cream from her hands. 'And there's no need to sound jealous. I don't know those women and I don't want to either.'

'I'm hardly *jealous*,' she snapped back, 'It's nothing to do with me. I'm merely stating the obvious. They find you attractive and they're letting you know it.'

'You know what's attractive?' he said, as he pooled the cream in his hands and rubbed it over her shoulders. 'You being jealous and not admitting it.'

She lifted her ponytail and said nothing, compliantly allowing him to rub cream down over the twin blades of her shoulders and along the rim of her bikini. The fine bones and the ripple of muscle under her skin was a soft-strong combination he found completely seductive.

'Your skin is flawless,' he whispered in her ear.

'Hmm…' she mumbled.

He bent lower and smoothed all the way down her bumpy spine, fanning his hands out to cover her back.

'I'll be getting a lot more of it these next few months.'

'More beautiful, then,' he said, and he popped a

little kiss on her warm cheek, lingering for a moment to savour the sensation of her hair and her ear as they brushed against him gently.

Oh, how he would have liked to linger there, he thought. But this was the exclusive Hotel St-Agnes, and she had already drawn her boundaries. Breaking them down was going to be a very enjoyable task.

He stood back and pulled off his T-shirt.

Twenty laps ought to cool things down for now.

He powered through the water, aware of the muffled voices of the children and the occasional snippet of conversation as he came up for air. Spending this time was a luxury he hadn't factored into this week. The aftermath of the Cordon d'Or was supposed to be spent tying up other bits of hospitality and calling in more favours.

He had some solid clients he needed to line up before he met with Arturo. Their influence would be crucial as he went forward with his negotiations. But all that was on hold because right now another plan was forming in his head.

Ruby was obviously pregnant. If he was lucky the media interest in him would soon have faded and no one would be any the wiser until after the event. But if he was unlucky, the ex-boyfriend of Lady Faye would still gather some mainstream press column space, and the last thing he needed was the media or the very devout Arturos casting aspersions on his character because of his pregnant girlfriend.

His mind was whirring with ideas and scenarios.

His stress level was pumping higher and higher. He could feel it, buzzing around his body. All the while he was caught up with Ruby, who knew what Claudio was plotting down in Saint Tropez? It was enough to drive him slowly out of his mind.

He hauled himself out of the water and sat on the edge of the pool, feeling sunbeams hot on his shoulders. Ahead, one of the topless women sat up on her elbows and lowered her sunglasses to stare. To his right, a waiter served Ruby a glass of water. She lifted the glass and beamed her beautiful smile in thanks. His eyes fell again to her blossoming figure. Their child was there, growing. This on top of everything else.

The timing was like a torrent. Everything was coming together and he could sink or swim.

He had to conduct this like the symphony of his life. Save the bank. Keep Claudio at bay. And find the best possible solution for the new baby that would soon be in the world. Of everything, he felt this the keenest of all. Because he would not let the child down. It was unthinkable.

'Hey, come on, I'll teach you a little water confidence,' he said, leaping up and walking towards her, dripping water all over the terrace.

Ruby looked up from her daydream and saw the man who filled her mind. He was everything every woman would want. His body was protector and warrior and lover all at once. Water droplets were coursing down from his shoulders over his pecs in the way her fingers had that night—joyously, greedily. The hair on his legs hugged every building muscle in wet tendrils. His shorts were soaked, outlining him, and she could feel herself respond.

She wanted him. As fiercely as she had wanted him that first time. Yes, she was jealous of those other women, and probably all of the other women to come, but right now—today—he was hers, and she was going to claim him.

'I can't swim,' she said, staring up at him.

'Did nobody ever teach you? Doesn't matter—it's just confidence. Come on.'

He reached for her hand and tugged her gently to her feet and she walked with him, feet slapping on the warm tiles, over to the edge of the pool. Steps disappeared into the blue water and she stood, looking at them.

'Come on, dancer girl. Try it.'

'I'm not sporty like you,' she said, pausing. 'You seem to be able to swim and sail and play rugby. The only thing I'm good at is dancing.'

'The only thing you've *tried* is dancing,' he corrected, and he was right. 'There's more to life than ballet. Come on—trust me.'

He stood beside her, held her hand in his as she walked down into the water, her feet slipping slightly on the mosaic tiles.

'All you have to do is get in all the way up to your waist…'

They walked together into the empty pool. She started to laugh. Thankfully the little children had all gone for shelter from the harsh midday sun. Only a couple of sun-worshippers remained, toasting their bronzed bodies on the loungers.

'And keep walking until it comes up to your chest. Feel good?'

The water was gloriously cooling on her hot skin, and his hand round hers was rough and strong.

'Oh, yes,' she said.

'Feel the water drag at your legs. Now, let's walk in a circle…just get used to how it feels. OK, now hold on to the edge of the pool and flutter your legs up.'

She clutched on to the edge and stretched herself out, kicking hard against the water.

'And soak me too—that's no problem at all,' he said, laughing.

She turned to see him covered in spray from where she had splash-kicked.

'Oh, I'm sorry!' she said, and automatically let go of the side to reach for him.

As she did so she slipped towards him, and he caught her, there against his chest, holding her safe in his arms. Their bodies slid together, wet and smooth, and then it happened. Eyes met. She saw his mouth open for her kiss. She put her arms around his neck as he lowered his head down and kissed her. His wet lips and wet face found hers and it wasn't a gentle kiss—not for long. It was a branding. It was a demanding mark that said she was his.

She felt it deep within her heart even as her brain called a little warning. She was getting in way over her head again. But she couldn't fight it—didn't want to. Words formed and died in her throat as she let the waves of passion pull her under, as she let his lips taste and his tongue plunder.

'We have to take this somewhere else,' he whispered, holding her close.

Her body was burning with sunshine and wet with water and passion, and she had to hold on or she felt she might slip out of his grasp and into the pool.

And then she was scooped up and into his arms, held taut against his chest as he walked them out of the pool.

'I seem to have this overwhelming urge to carry you. What the hell *is* this? I can promise you I've never lifted another woman before, and yet I seem to have carried you three times now. And counting.'

He waded out of the water and up the steps and she didn't care if anyone was watching. It felt too good to hold on, to be nestled against the wall of this man.

But when he didn't stop at their spot near the pool she lifted her head. 'Where are we going?'

'We're going to take a little holiday, like I said. Beginning right now.'

They were inside the airy hotel foyer now. She could feel the water cooling on her skin.

'*Madame* needs to lie down for a little while. In

the Presidential Suite. Arrange for our luggage to be transferred, please.'

Discreet staff opened doors. His footsteps sounded dull and heavy on carpet. The light changed from bright to soft. Sounds were muffled, then disappeared altogether as the door of the vast room closed behind them.

'Shower first,' he said, his voice a gravelly growl.

Still carrying her, he walked them through to the bathroom. It was decorated as if from a previous century. Pale pink tiles and towels and white ceramics. Brass feet and taps. The shower was over the bath, encircled in a white curtain, and it was there that she found herself standing as warm water began to drizzle and then pour over her body.

She looked at him, his dark hair drying in waves around his face, a smear of stubble on his jaw, and hunger in his brown berry eyes.

'You drive me wild, woman,' he said.

'Just how wild do you mean?' she asked, staring at his shoulders and his chest, and at the forest of hair that ran across it and down to his shorts.

And then he put his hands on them and tugged them down. She bit her lip at the sight of his magnificent arousal.

There was no way to stop now, even if she wanted to.

'*That* wild?' she said. 'May I?'

She dropped to her knees and held him in her hands. Water slid over her back and she slipped slightly on the surface of the bath in her rush to have the whole of him in her mouth.

He groaned aloud as she suckled him, her lips and tongue tugging furiously, somehow knowing just how to drive him on. Her other hand gripped his buttock and pulled him closer still. And she felt her power, was invigorated by it. Emboldened.

'Ruby, please. You have to stop.'

She pulled back, still licking and sucking, her eyes roaming up his fierce body to his dark tortured gaze. Then he reached for her and she was lifted to her feet. He undid her bikini top and released her tender breasts. Her nipples were erect and he put his lips to one, gently.

'Is this OK? Not too painful?'

She bit back a whimper and shook her head.

'Pain like this I can take all day long,' she said.

'Take these off. I want to see all of you. See if I had you right in my dreams.'

She paused as she shimmied out of her bikini briefs.

'You were dreaming about me?' she whispered mischievously.

He smiled that little half-smile and looked almost bashful.

She held his head in her hands, ran her fingers through the thick shock of hair, emboldened by each moment.

'Tell me. Were you dreaming about me?'

'Once or twice,' he answered, smiling up into her

eyes. 'Probably not as much as *you* were dreaming about me, though.'

'I never gave you a second thought.'

He lathered soap in his hands, began to stroke all over her body, warming her and washing her.

'I didn't make much of an impression?'

She felt his hands slide over her tummy, her breasts, then gently in between her legs.

Her head fell back as he slid his clever fingers slowly backwards and forwards, rubbing exactly where she was swollen and longing for his touch. The sound of his hands slipping and sliding on her wet, naked body brought every bundled nerve screaming to life.

Then he cradled her in one arm and laid her over his lap. Her legs fell open and he slipped his fingers into the very apex of her thighs and kept up an insistent pressure while he lowered his head and thrust his tongue into her mouth.

And just like that she orgasmed—fully, powerfully, and with a suddenness that shook her to the very centre of her being.

She writhed and jerked and screamed. 'Oh, Matteo...oh, my God,' she called as the shock waves left her.

And then she was wrapped in a towel and carried through to the bedroom. Slowly he dried her, and kissed her drying skin, and then he knelt before her, proudly aroused and ready.

She sat up on her elbows, her mouth open in shocked delight.

'Is it all coming back to you now?' He smiled as he leaned over her, stretched his arms out, encircling her with his body.

'That you have the woman of your dreams at your mercy?'

He chuckled. 'You never give up!'

He nudged her legs open with his knee.

'I never do. I'm what people call "driven".'

'You're driving me insane right now, Ruby. That's for sure.'

And he thrust himself inside her and she watched as his face registered the pleasure. And then she felt it herself, as she hugged her legs around him and let go of all her cares and worries and fears as it became only her and him and nothing else.

CHAPTER FOURTEEN

'THIS PLACE IS AMAZING. I'd no idea these little islands existed. How did you discover them?' asked Ruby, sliding a forkful of delicious salad into her mouth and chewing happily.

It was dinnertime, and she was starving. They'd made love all afternoon and dozed until the sun began to dip and the light flooding into the sumptuous suite had turned from bright yellow to a gauzy orange.

His body was hers and her body was his. That was all she knew. She ached for him in a way she'd never believed was possible, but now, replete in his arms, she was aware of her mind starting to chatter its warnings. But she would not listen. She would not let those thoughts take hold.

Not yet.

She gazed across the candlelit table to where Matteo sat, lost in that world he disappeared into so often. His hair was swept back from his face and his smooth brow was gathered in a frown. The white shirt he wore was collarless, dipping low to the shadow of his chest, and loose enough to lend him the appearance of a brooding long-ago hero. She'd never seen him look more handsome.

He nodded out to the bay. 'We did a lot of sailing when I was younger. There's not an inch of these waters we haven't been to at one time or another, the three of us—my mother and father and me.'

'Is there any sport you *don't* do?' she asked.

It was a flippant comment, and she almost regretted it, but his mood was slipping into serious waters and she still didn't want to navigate them. It was as if he was building up to say something. And she wasn't quite ready to hear it.

Even if they both walked away from today, they would be forced back together many times in the future. What kind of relationship would they have? One with hot sex and then flights in opposite directions? Or would he cut it dead and dread the thought of seeing her again? File her under 'No Further Action'.

Heart flipping and stomach churning, she forced a bright smile. They had to have a serious talk. She'd been pushing for it since this morning, but now that the moment was here she didn't want to spoil things. She wanted to keep the illusion going a little longer.

'Well? You swim...you play rugby. You box...'

He was looking steadily at her. He raised an eyebrow. 'I don't do ballet,' he said.

She caught the momentary flash of fun in his eyes

and smiled back. 'Our child will. Especially if he's a boy. It'll be the making of him.'

'Now, that's an interesting thought.' He smiled. 'And will you be one of those overbearing mothers, berating the coach, or whatever they're called, because Matty Junior didn't get picked for the role of Sugar Plum Fairy?'

'You mean the ballet master,' she corrected him. 'And, yes, very probably. Don't tell me you won't be shouting at Little Miss Ruby from the touchline? What's good for the goose...'

'I can see we're going to have some interesting times ahead,' he replied, but it was quietly said, as if he was lost in other thoughts.

He touched his glass with his finger. There it was—his sign that he was ready to speak.

Well, all right. It had to come at some point.

She put down her knife and fork and waited for him to start. The restaurant was quiet, save for the sounds of the touch of silverware on china and muted conversation in the very best French. But still he remained silent, staring at the leaves on his plate.

'Not eating anything?' she asked, nodding to his untouched food. 'Or drinking? Don't you want any wine? You don't need to hold back on my account.'

'No. I've given up alcohol,' he said, and the ghost of his smile slid and died.

'For what? For health reasons? You're the healthiest guy I know. Surely a little wine won't do you any harm?'

He shook his head. 'There's a lot about me that you don't know. And you probably need to know if we're going to go into this thing together.'

Her ears pricked up at the word 'thing'. Her heart swelled with fear and hope in equal measures. And it was then, in that moment, that she realised that more than anything else she wanted to spend more time with him. Not just parenting time, but real time. Friends time and lovers time.

But he was a man who didn't commit. And she would never, ever beg any man for anything.

'My father had a difficult relationship with alcohol...'

He was staring at nothing, touching his glass again. The light from the candle flickered, daubing his face with ochre shadows, hollowing and saddening his features.

'I didn't know how difficult it was until he died. He could go for weeks, months, without it, but when he got the taste he couldn't stop. It was like a demon inside, him making him drink until he had drunk everything dry.'

'Your poor mother,' was all she could say, suddenly imagining a young Mrs Rossini, her face troubled with pain.

He nodded absently at that. 'My mother could do nothing when he got like that—he didn't even know who she was. But he battled it. He went to rehab clinics. Three times. He took it head-on and he sorted himself out. We're fighters, me and him—

you know?' he said, spearing her with a sudden look in the half-light.

She didn't know what to do with that look. She didn't know what he was saying—was he reassuring her? Warning her?

'But then the bank got into trouble and started losing clients. He didn't know why at the time, and for months he held it together...'

His face changed, saddened, and he dropped his head. It was as if her heart was being squeezed. To see such a man, so virile and strong and—kind...

She reached across the table for his hand, instinctively, and he looked up with surprise.

'But you're not like that,' she said, and then cautiously, 'Are you?'

'No, I'm not,' he said, and he drew his hand away and sat up straight, giving her a look right in the eyes. 'And I'm not going to risk it happening to me either. If I go down, the whole thing sinks. Banca Casa di Rossini is two hundred years old. And we're still struggling to recover from the sabotage that happened all those years ago.'

'I thought your bank was flourishing? You have all these things—a jet and a boat and... Are you saying you're not...rich?'

It was the worst thing in the world to say. She sounded callous and selfish, but how could she avoid it?

He looked sharply at her. 'I am very rich and I intend to stay that way. I have responsibilities. As well as this baby I have my mother and my family name. The bank, the people who work for me. There's a merger almost on the table and I won't let anything get in the way of that.'

'I don't doubt you for a minute,' she said quietly. 'But what could go wrong? Are you saying that our baby is going to get in the way of your merger?'

'You saw those recent pictures in the press—us together, and me with other women—pictures from the past ten years? That was set up by someone who wants to discredit me and make me look like some kind of sex addict. Now, with you pregnant, they'll try to dig up even more dirt. And old Arturo isn't going to get into bed with a philandering sex addict.'

She sat back, her mind racing. 'Who's behind this?'

He shook his head and frowned. 'It's a long story. A guy called Claudio Calvaneo. My father's business partner.

His fingers clasped the glass tightly and he looked up at her, and it was such a penetrating look that she was held there, transfixed in his gaze.

'I'm going to need your help, Ruby.'

'To do what? This is way out of my league.'

He shook his head. 'The merger has to be handled with kid gloves. I've already had a first meeting and we're going to meet again very soon. All being well, there will be even more meetings in the coming months.'

She scanned his eyes as her brain raced to keep

up with him, but his face was set in that expression-less cast of rock again.

'Arturo's already seen you with me—thanks to Claudio's smear—and the minute there's a whisper that you're pregnant the whole thing could come down like a house of cards unless we have our story sorted.'

'You need to spell this out for me. I'm not really following.'

'He needs to see me as a serious guy, if he's going to entrust his company to me—someone who's sober and sincere about life and money. I can't be the kind of guy who gets a woman pregnant and then doesn't do the right thing. His bank means as much to him as Casa di Rossini does to us. More. It's the child he never had.'

The restaurant was now completely silent. Every-one had retired to other rooms and only a lone waiter moved through the space with a tray of glasses. Mat-teo's eyes tracked him as he exited, and then swung round to her, pinning her with his stare.

'I want him to think that we are more than just a casual fling. I want him to think that we are commit-ted to one another, building a life together.'

'By "building a life" you mean…?'

'Totally committed to one another and our child. Marriage.'

'Marriage?' she blurted, and half-laughed, caught out by shock. 'Marriage—as in…?'

'I know what I'm asking of you is above and

beyond—we barely know one another. But you're carrying my child. And I'm fighting for my life here—for many lives. This merger will see the bank in great financial shape—no one will need to worry about money again.'

He was up now, on his feet, leaning towards her. His shirt fell open, revealing a glimpse of his chest, and his scent hung like warm velvet on a cold night, wrapping around her, drawing her in.

'This isn't just for my future. It's for our child too.'

She shook her head in disbelief. This was too much to take in.

He was so close she could see tiny amber flecks in his eyes and the sleek lines of the eyelashes that encased them. His thick brown brows were knit in anticipation.

'I know I'm throwing this at you—asking you to take me on trust...'

'I can't get my head round this. You need to give me time to think.'

'There isn't any time. We have to do it *now*.'

'But how would it work? Not that I'm saying I will, but—'

He dropped to his knee and held her hands. 'I've worked it out. It's perfect. We can be married before the end of the week. Tiny, private—we can release a picture and take a few days' honeymoon, and then we'll head to Arturo's villa next weekend. You'll absolutely charm him. All his doubts will be gone.'

'But *marriage*,' she said. 'It's—massive. It's not

something you can pretend, or turn off like a tap. What happens after next weekend? When I go back to London and you go back to work? There's no way we can keep it a secret then.'

'I'm not worried about after—that'll sort itself out. Whatever you want to do—I'm with you. But this is the single most important event of my professional career. This way the bank will be intact—not just for me, and our baby, but for his or her children too. Casa di Rossini will go on for years. My family will be secure.'

He was going so fast, was flying with ideas. She had to stop and think and be sure. She couldn't make the wrong choice now. It was the hugest decision of her life. Everything from here on in, every future step, hung on this moment.

'But there are other ways to be secure—and our child might not *want* to be a private banker. What then?'

He looked at her as if she was completely mad, as if she'd spoken in a different language, and she saw that he had no concept of anything other than his way of life. It was ingrained so deeply within him that all other choices were completely moot. And he wanted to drag her into it too.

She thought about her own path, how deeply she had been prepared to plough her own furrow, blinkered and refusing to see any other way.

'Matteo, maybe—just maybe—this should be left

to fate to decide. You've been trying so hard for so long and maybe—'

'I can't leave this to fate. Not until I've tried every single thing I can do. And this—you being pregnant. I thought it was a disaster, but now I think it might just be the best thing for all of us.'

She narrowed her eyes. 'What do you mean?'

'I mean that having this added responsibility has made me even more focused. I thought Dad was going to live for another thirty years or more. I knew I was probably going to take charge—it was always hanging over me—but it seemed way off in the distance. Even when he died I really struggled to accept that this was my life now. But you…the baby. I know how my world has to be. I have to make this work. Don't you see?'

She opened her mouth but he shook his head and walked away, and there, framed in the restaurant window, he looked so terribly alone, set apart in his own tormented world.

And she had walked right into the middle of it. Could she leave him alone with this? She needed him as much as he needed her. Maybe even more. But this—this went beyond anything she had imagined.

Her head hurt as she tried to think. But her heart was sure. Even if it had been trampled in the process. Because how could she keep herself safe from falling in love with him? It was already be too late…

'What exactly do you need me to do next weekend?'

He spun around from the window. And suddenly he looked warrior-proud, invincible.

'Act like you love me.'

She felt a savage squeeze to her heart as his words made her gasp, and her eyes burned hot with tears. She bit her lip, forced her chin to steady. She kept her face to the floor, desperately clawing back her composure, furious at her own weakness.

He was totally oblivious. He moved closer still. Energy rolled off him in waves. She crossed her arms over her body, rubbed her fingers on her bare flesh.

'It doesn't have to be true, Ruby. I'm not asking for the world. But when you came to see me you wanted to force me to acknowledge the situation. You wanted me to give you cast-iron guarantees that I would play my part. Well, now I am prepared to admit that I will. I will give you way more than you wanted.'

'I only ever wanted one thing in my life,' she said, 'I only ever wanted my career and you need to know that that is still what I want. You're not seeing *my* needs in all this.'

He shook his head and moved right in front of her. The rest of the room—the view of the gardens through the half-closed roman blinds, the masts of the yachts and their white blooming sails, the world beyond—was blocked out. It was hard to think, to remember who she was and what she was, when he was so close.

'Ruby, you can have everything. *Everything.* Don't you want to marry me?'

'I'm not saying no, but does it have to be this way?' she pleaded. 'Do we have to be married to convince Arturo that you're the right person to take this merger forward? People have children together and live apart all the time.'

'He's very religious—for him there's no other way to raise a child but in wedlock, under the eyes of God.'

'But we would be living a lie—isn't that worse?'

'To give our child the stability it needs is *worse*? We'll sign a pre-nup. You'll get a house and a car and an income. As soon as the merger is secure we can decide what happens next. Where you live and what you do. A nanny. My name. All of that.'

His words were cold, transactional, black and white. There was no emotion or love or kindness or care. His heart was invested in his bank, in his dead father's memory, in a future that he didn't even want for himself.

And now she was a part of it too.

As she stared out at the balmy summer Côte D'Azur evening a chill of loneliness spread over her as damp and dark as all those nights in that frozen Croydon flat. The spectre was still there, whispering in her ear that she might *think* she had it all worked out, she might be *imagining* some shiny new future. But money didn't kill loneliness. Oh, no. She couldn't buy her way out this. It was only love that could do that.

Love that she feared and craved in equal measures. Love that had been like a forbidden fruit—just out of reach. The fleeting glimpse of her mother's smile, the squeeze of a passing hug. Those momentary touches that had spread sunlight through her and then been washed away, because there had never been enough to go round.

So she'd turned to the rapture of an audience and the warm delight of an aching body that performed perfection for them and the chance that maybe some day in that sea of faces, her father would call out her name Because that kept the sunshine there that little bit longer.

And now she wanted more. She wanted to feel Matteo's love. She wanted to love and be loved in return. Marry him, live with him, have a child with him. Dance. And maybe, just maybe, be a good mum…

She wanted to know how it felt to be loved for herself. Not for her smile, or her long dark hair, or her clever body. She wanted to be loved for being *Ruby*.

CHAPTER FIFTEEN

HE LET THE car window slide slowly down, then cut the engine. Warm, humid air pushed against his face and he reached for his collar, tugged the knot of his tie loose and flicked at the top button until it popped open.

Suits. He still hated wearing them and couldn't accept that he'd become one. Still never properly saw himself as that type. He'd hated being made to wear one as a teenager. Being choked in the suffocating confines of grey gabardine had *not* been his idea of a good time.

And he'd managed to avoid wearing them right up until his father's funeral. By then there had been no choice—and how much worse could it have been anyway? He'd started learning to fill his father's shoes before the hard, lumpy earth was scattered on his coffin, and he was still learning. Still a work in progress.

He got out and stretched his legs. The drive up from London had been sweet and smooth, and he was just in the mood for a little wander round the lake and then up to the house where the British Ballet held their summer school. And where his beautiful wife-to-be would be waiting to meet him.

He lifted his jacket from the back seat, slung it over his shoulder and began to move along the driveway towards the patch of blue lake, lying flat and still like a bright blue eye in a green face.

A flurry of girls just like a little Ruby flew past him down the sweep of stone steps, hair scraped back in buns and slim as flamingos. He tried to work out their age. Six? Seven? He had very little idea when it came to things like that. He had very little idea about children at all, but after years of regarding them as something he could barely tolerate, the idea of a little Ruby to cherish almost felled him at the knees.

He couldn't imagine anything sweeter. To think that his child would be born innocent, helpless and dependent on him, was almost drowning out every other waking thought. He felt like a warrior for this unborn child. He would do anything and everything he could for the little bundle of soft bones and tiny developing organs he had seen on the scan with Ruby yesterday.

His little girl.

For years he'd positioned himself as a confirmed bachelor. How he'd scoffed at other men, scorned their happy family weekend stories, derided the doting daddy photographs in their wallets. He'd been superior to all that. He'd never get caught out. He was too damn smart.

But when he'd seen that image...

Life would never be the same again. He was sure of that. He only wished he could be so sure of Ruby.

He'd watched her at the scan, lying on the bed. As the consultant had put the image on the screen he'd watched her eyes flicker and widen with surprise. She'd turned pale, and her mouth had tightened into a worried line, her hands into fists. If he hadn't known any better he'd have said she was terrified. But that didn't make any sense. Women *loved* babies.

He'd tried to hold her hand, but she'd pulled it away. He'd tried again—reached out to touch her stomach—but she'd literally flinched.

He'd tried to jolly her along after the consultant had left the room, but it had seemed as if she was caught in a trance. And unable and unwilling to jump out of it.

They'd travelled back to the penthouse in a silence punctuated only by the business calls he'd had to take—calls he'd been able to do nothing about, stoking the flames of the Arturo deal, keeping the embers warm so he could pick it up again after the weekend. How could he not? And as he'd done so he had felt her moving further and further away— as if she was walking away from him in a blizzard, swallowed up into another world, hidden from sight, muffled, unreachable.

He'd insisted on the scan the moment they'd arrived back from Ile-St-Agnes. He'd thought it would bring them closer—he'd thought wrong. He'd assumed she'd move in with him immediately—but no. In the three days since they'd got back they were still working on that. She wanted to stay independent, living in her little flat until they left to be married, even though that was only in two days' time.

So all he could do was wait. And plan. And hope that in these moments when the enormity of it all reared up like a wall of men battling in a scrum—a force so physical that he felt he might be crushed, as if with one wrong move, one moment of weakness the whole thing could go—all he could do was pray. Because he'd never have the energy to fight like this again. There would never be another chance, when everything was laid out for him. It was now or never.

They were going straight from here—Birch Lodge, the beautiful old manor house set in its own grounds in the north of London, where the youngest British Ballet dancers boarded and attended lessons—to the airport, and then on to be married in private in Rome.

There would be a few guests—his closest friends, as well as his mother and David. Ruby hadn't wanted to invite anyone, and nothing he'd done to try and persuade her to talk about her father or contact her mother had succeeded.

It was a strange relationship, he had to admit. They seemed to be as distant and he and his own mother were close. But he wasn't going to judge.

How could he? As long as Ruby and the baby were OK, his mother had enough love to go round.

He turned from the still, glassy lake as another flurry of movement caught his eye. This time the children were definitely older—early teens. Boys and girls. He watched them, curious to see their fresh-faced youth, their lithe, strong bodies. He probably hadn't looked much different himself once...

'Matteo!'

He looked round at the sound of her voice and there she was. And, God help him, even at thirty paces he could feel the punch of that smile like a squeeze on his heart. Because now he could read it. He could see that it wasn't full and free. It was a smile of greeting, but not of welcome. She could smile brighter and better and bolder than anyone he had ever met, but there was always something held back, something hiding behind it.

But when she really smiled—when he made love to her and she lay warm in his arms, when she forgot all about her troubles and he saw who she really was—that was when he felt as if he had pulled her back from the blizzard and brought her indoors, set her by the fire. And he'd watch as the roses bloomed in her cheeks and the sparkle shone from her eyes.

'Hi,' he said, striding over the grass towards her, never taking his eyes from her where she stood on the top step, looking down at him.

She opened her arms wide—gracefully, hypnotically. 'Beautiful day,' she said, indicating the grounds.

'Even more beautiful now,' he said, walking right up to her and putting his arms around her, folding her to him and loving the way she melded into him so perfectly. Their bodies, so different, somehow fitted together like two halves of a whole. He placed a kiss on her cheek, and then on the other, and then, because he wanted more and he didn't care who saw, he took one from her lips.

She smiled. 'I have a reputation to maintain here, you know.'

'I know,' he said, tucking her under his arm and walking them down the steps. 'How were your classes today?'

'I'm getting to really like it. Having all those little faces staring at me, trying to help them without criticising… And the feeling when they get it right is amazing. Almost as good as dancing itself.'

'You must be a natural.'

'Oh, I'm not a natural—far from it. I just love dancing and so do they.'

Just then the crowd of little girls came rushing up the grass, back from their afternoon break. They crowded around Ruby, jumping up and down, giggling excitedly.

'Where are you going?'

'Are you coming back tomorrow?'

'Please come back and teach us again—we had so much fun.'

And then they all swarmed off, like a cloud of starlings.

'You see, you're a natural,' he said solemnly, nodding and then he squeezed her hand to underline his message. 'Just like you're going to be with our little one.'

They walked towards the car, and he felt her fingers weaken in his grip as silence descended around them again. But he wasn't going to let it take hold of her. He was going to power through. He could not afford for her to get cold feet.

'We're all set for the weekend. We'll go from here to the airport and land in Rome about seven. My mother will arrive about midnight, so you won't see her until tomorrow. Ceremony's set for eleven…'

He paused, stole a quick glance at her over the roof of the car. But her face was hidden behind huge sunglasses and her mouth gave nothing away.

'I spoke with Augusto this afternoon, too. We're expected there next Friday, by which point we'll be married…'

She was pulling her seat belt across her body with infinite care. He started the engine and nosed the car along the driveway.

'Which is just as well because it turns out Claudio is going to visit them immediately after us.'

He turned sharply to look at her, to see her reaction. There was none.

'So anything he tries to say—any dirt he tries to dish up—we'll have covered all the bases. We'll play the happiest, cutest newlyweds this side of the Apennine Mountains. And there's nothing Arturo loves more than a young Italian family and all that promises to follow. Kids and houses and happily-ever-after.'

He turned again to see her, but she had turned her head to stare out of the window.

He reached for her hand, squeezed it. 'Everything OK?'

'Yes, of course. Obviously I want to get back to work as soon as I can. Now that I'm getting into it I really don't want to go disappearing for long.'

'Obviously,' he said, turning resolutely back to face the road. 'It should all be tied up one way or the other in about ten days. That's not too long to be away, is it? It *is* your wedding, after all.'

They rolled along in silence but he could hear her thinking as clear as day.

It's not a real wedding, though, is it?

And he knew that. He knew it all the way from his overloaded brain down to the sick feeling in the pit of his stomach. What he was doing was wrong. It was wrong to make her do this. It was wrong to bind her to him like this because he wanted this merger so badly.

But, more than that, he wanted his little family.

Yes, he did.

He wanted his little girl and he wanted her mother. And he was prepared to do anything to get it—because he had to. He had to make this work.

He had to move those wheels, push all those pieces into position himself.

It was the long game—and he'd been playing it his whole life. If he didn't push on with this, then what? The bank would sink into oblivion and this woman would disappear off and some other guy would marry her.

No!

He slammed the steering wheel with his open hand so suddenly that the car veered slightly off the road and Ruby turned round, alarmed.

'What's wrong?'

'I'm sorry—I didn't mean to do that.' He shook his head, furious at his lack of composure. He could not allow cracks to show. Not anger, not alcohol, nothing. 'Ruby, I really want this to work.'

'I know you do.'

'No, I mean *really*. I really want this to work. It would mean the world to me. I've never properly come out and said it, but I can't get it out of my head. You and the baby. The bank. Everything.'

'There's no reason why it shouldn't,' she said quietly. 'You've done everything you could.'

He heard the wistful tone in her voice. The note of self-sacrifice was like a soprano's aria, cutting through the crystal of his own determination. She was sacrificing everything for him and their baby. Her career was effectively over for months. All she could do was cling on to the company by teaching at the school.

And what of them? Of their relationship? It was as vulnerable and beautiful and new as the baby growing inside her. He would do anything to nurture it and bring it fully to life. He wanted to do the right thing for Ruby, but that meant doing this first. Doing his duty. Once all that was dealt with, then he could finally relax…

'You know this won't last for ever,' he said, trying to cheer her up. 'We'll come out the other side and get back on track with our lives.'

'Yes, I know.'

'I won't hold you back, Ruby. I want you to be happy too. I want both of us to get what we want out of this. Your career, the bank secure, Claudio a distant memory—all of it.'

'And you really think that your having the biggest, most successful private bank in Europe is going to make Claudio disappear? Don't you think that if the merger goes ahead he'll find even more reasons to hate you? From what you've told me about him, I think he'll make it his life's work to destroy your bank. This isn't going to make him go away—it's going to make him worse.'

Matteo frowned and shook his head as he spotted the signs for the airport and turned off.

'No,' he said, dismissing the thought. 'He'll leave well alone. And anyway—this isn't about him. This is about doing the right thing for the Rossinis. I've got to get the bank—'

'Back to where it was,' she finished for him, in a resigned voice. 'I know. I get it. I just wish *you* did.'

She'd muttered the last words under her breath, but he'd caught them. Why was she being like this? His plan was sound—solid. Why was she poking holes in the one thing that he knew was completely right?

He parked the car, cut the engine and got out. He walked round the other side to help her out, but she was on her feet and had slammed the door already.

Hearing the roar of the jets and feeling the warm summer wind whipping at his face, he followed her into the building.

'I don't expect you to see it like I do, Ruby. Nobody can know what it has been like.'

In the cool air-conditioned lobby she spun to face him. 'You were a *rugby player*, for God's sake, Matteo. You're only a banker because you were forced to be, and you're never going to be free of this until you give it up. Just give it up! You're running face-first into a wall that you've built for yourself when you should be running in the opposite direction.'

She pulled her sunglasses off as she spoke and he saw tears in her eyes and anger pinching at her mouth.

'I don't need you to marry me. I can cope perfectly well without all this. I'll get by—you don't need to give it a second thought on my account.'

'What are you talking about? When did I ever give you the impression that I don't want to do this?

You've got it totally wrong. This is bigger than both of us. I don't have any choice. There *is* no choice!'

As he said the words he heard himself. But there *was* no choice. There wasn't…

'There's always a choice,' she said quietly. 'You just can't see it.'

The nose of a jet pushed into view on the Tarmac. Three uniformed staff in pristine navy and white walked past, trundling little carry-on cases. His phone buzzed in his pocket. He turned away and pulled it out.

'David,' he said. 'What's up?'

'I thought you'd want to know. Your stock has just gone up—I've heard from the Levinson Group that they've finished with Claudio's operation and they're moving back to us. And with them will come others. You're in a really strong position now to go into the final stages of negotiation with Arturo. But you'll need to come back as soon as you can to keep this moving. Can you do a dinner tonight? And some meetings on Monday? I know you wanted me to keep a few days free for your little holiday, but this is all happening now and we can't afford to miss a trick.'

'Great—of course I can. That's amazing,' he said, looking at the retreating back of Ruby, at the long ponytail defining the perfect symmetry of her perfect body.

Her posture was graceful and proud in every movement. She smiled as she handed her passport to the ground crew, and her eyes, as they flicked to him, held that secret dark promise that he still couldn't read.

And he was going to marry her. He was going to marry that woman because he damned well wanted to have her in his life. He wanted to be with her. It made him feel good. It made him feel happy and hopeful and as if there was a point to life.

Things were coming together. A beautiful, perfect fit. He was going to pull this off. He was going to be a father.

He was going to be a husband.

CHAPTER SIXTEEN

THERE WASN'T A sound when Ruby woke for the third time, alone in the antique brass bed, swaddled in the finest cream linen sheets. She'd barely slept, but already the brightening tones of morning were pushing against the windows and seeping in through the heavy drapes. She reached an arm out to check the time on her phone. Six a.m. Five hours to go.

Five hours until her life changed irrevocably—though hadn't it changed already? Hadn't it changed the moment she'd put on that red dress, opened that bottle of beer and shared the story of Rumi's poetry on that flight from Rome to London with the most wonderful man in the world? There was no going back from that moment—because that was when she had fallen completely and hopelessly in love with him.

Nothing else and no one else would ever have induced her to step from her path—her blinkered, stubborn path that had been going nowhere other than forward into loneliness. But at least then she had known every step—she had been sure where her foot would land, where her path would eventually lead.

Now she was on some slippery path, in a changing landscape that made her feel giddy with excitement one minute and sick with dread the next. So she was marrying him—she was going to do the one thing that Lady Faye had wanted more than anything else. But they weren't marrying for love. They were marrying for the sake of a baby. And a bank.

She traced the patterns on the ceiling with her eyes. The ceiling of the room that from here on forward would be her bedroom in Rome. In a house that she would never have been able to afford as a dancer—even as the prima ballerina in one of the world's best companies. Even as a director...

From along the hallway the noises of the day started to sound. Unfamiliar voices were talking in an unfamiliar language. They hadn't seen a soul last night when they'd arrived at his home. The flight had been short but the dinner with Matteo's clients had been long—delicious, but long—and despite his apologies, and his thanks for agreeing to the last-minute change of plan, she'd felt exhausted when he'd finally slid the key in the lock of his Roman villa and they'd quietly made their way to bed.

He'd made love to her. Romantically, passionately, adoringly. And then he'd slipped off to another room for the sake of tradition—as if their marriage was somehow real. As if she was going to have something old and new, borrowed and blue too. And a father to give her away, a mother to weep, and bridesmaids to throw her bouquet to. And a happily-ever-after.

The wincing pain of self-pity cut at her, making her crush her eyes closed. Because even though she'd been in denial about her deepest wishes, now that they were finally coming true she wanted even more.

But she was here in Rome, healthy and comfortable and with more choices than she'd ever had before in her life. She could work, rest, have the baby, then go back to work, back to dance.

The only thing she couldn't do was make Matteo love her. Or make him love himself.

There was another noise now—closer, outside the door.

'Prendo che. I'll take that.'

She strained to listen and had just figured out that it was Coral Rossini's voice when the door was opened and in came the lady herself, carrying a tray.

Ruby sat bolt-upright, totally shocked by the interruption. She'd known she would have to see her new mother-in-law at some point—but *now*? Like *this*…?

'Good morning, Ruby!' She came right into the room, put the tray down and opened first one set of curtains, then the other. 'Sleep well?'

Ruby pulled back the sheet and tried to get out of bed.

'No, no, stay there—you have to have breakfast in bed.'

Coral Rossini picked up the tray and came over to the bed, the fresh morning light streaming in to reveal the golden glow from the African sun on her well-tended skin and eyes that were penetratingly bright and clear.

Ruby watched her warily. What was her tone going to be? Would she hate her, thinking that she had trapped her beloved son? Would she be cool and condescending? Or the same old Coral who had sparkled and charmed every other time she'd seen her?

She put the tray down and sat beside it on the bed, her gaze never shifting. 'It's your wedding day—and I'm here to look after you. But first,' she said, 'let's have a proper chat.' She poured tea from a modern silver pot, one cup each. 'Milk?' she asked.

Ruby nodded, sat up straighter, took the cup, cleared her throat and said, 'Thanks…'

'Well, I'll bet neither of us could have imagined we'd be here a few weeks ago. But here we are.'

'Coral, I want you to know that I really and truly did not mean for any of this to happen. I hope you don't think…'

The older woman sat back and looked at her carefully. 'No. I don't think. So just stop there. I have known you since you were a teenager—since Banca Casa di Rossini started to sponsor the company and I started coming to see you and all your lovely friends rehearsing and performing and pushing yourselves to the limit. I know what dancing means to you.'

Coral reached for her hand.

'I know, Ruby,' she said, quietly. 'I know your mother moved away. And I don't want to pry, but everyone needs a mother and I'll be yours, for as long as you want me to be.'

Ruby felt her throat burn and her eyes sting as she choked back the surge of emotion that gushed forth inside her. She pursed her lips hard and nodded. 'Thanks,' she said, returning the squeeze on her fingers.

'It's my pleasure. Just love my grandchild and love my son. Don't assume that they won't need you, because they will. They *will*. And we won't give up on you. We're your family now.'

Ruby stared at her. How did she know? How did this woman know that her biggest fear in the world was that they would give up on her because they'd realise, like everyone else did, that there was something unlovable about her? How could Coral open her mouth and say aloud the words that she, Ruby, couldn't even bear to think?

What was she going to do if it all fell apart?

In ten short days she'd gone from being terrified that she would be left alone to look after a baby to feeling terrified that Matteo would realise he could do it all without her.

All her life she'd been so sure that she could tough it out alone, but the moment Matteo had walked into her life nothing had felt sure any more. She'd thrown caution to the wind and slept with him, and now she was pregnant by him and getting married. Her rules and boundaries were looser than the curtains wafting in the breeze.

'I know,' Coral said, sipping her tea but never taking

her eyes from her, 'that had things been different—the baby, this merger with Arturo—we might not be sitting where we are right now. But Matteo is very fond of you. I've no doubt about that. And what you're going to do today shows me that you are very fond of him too.'

Ruby stared at Coral, desperately keen to tell her just how much he meant to her…how he made her feel alive…how he understood her like no one had ever taken the trouble to do before. How he'd made her begin to feel strong and sure and confident about raising a child.

'He'll be a great dad,' she said. 'He'll do everything for the baby.'

'Exactly,' said Coral, smiling. 'That's exactly what I think too.'

They sipped their tea in silence for another moment. Then Coral spoke again.

'Family is very important to us. Your child—my grandchild—is going to be brought up in a loving family. And you, lovely, sweet Ruby, are going to be part of that loving family'

Then she lifted the cup and saucer, lifted the tray, put it down carefully on the floor and enveloped her in the firmest, surest hug. And Ruby felt something thaw in the deepest, coldest corner of her heart. She squeezed her back, sealing a heartfelt promise and knowing that another little sliver of rainbow had spread its colour in her life.

'Now, let's get you looking even more beautiful. If that's possible.'

* * *

Calvaneo Capital's London headquarters sat on the top ten floors of one of the tallest skyscrapers in Canary Wharf. The lift was fast and efficient, and already crowded with people in the uniform navy and grey of the world's financial elite. It was eight a.m. GMT. Three hours before Matteo was due to make his vows in Rome.

He was in no mood be kept waiting.

He stepped out at the fiftieth floor and made his way to the reception area. He stood out from the throng, as he always did, his hair longer, a foot taller, broader. But it wasn't just his body that set him apart today. The white rose and the morning suit raised eyebrows and smiles in his wake.

He had phoned ahead, left a message, so the shape of Claudio coming along the teak-floored, glass-walled corridor towards him was no surprise. But the sight of him still made his heart pump and his fists clench and bile rise in his throat.

'Matteo. How kind of you to drop by.'

He looked older, his skin lined, but well preserved. The hair slicked back from his face was a peppery grey, where it had once been black, and his jacket was buttoned over a paunch where before there had been a well-defined six-pack. But other than that he was exactly the same.

'This isn't a casual call, Claudio. As you can see I'm getting married later today, so I won't be long.'

He walked straight past Claudio to the doorway

he'd seen him emerge from. The gold letters of his name etched in the glass confirmed it as the CEO's office. He walked right in and looked around.

It was a room for entertaining as much as business, laid out like a nineteen-twenties lounge, with overstuffed stylised furniture, beautiful objects and silver-framed photographs of the rich and the beautiful, clients and friends.

He turned around. 'For someone who's stock is spiralling out of control, you're looking remarkably calm. But then you're used to bad news, being the cause of so much of it.'

'You came all this way to tell me how calm I look? Why, thank you. You look very well too. Very handsome. Your father would be proud. I feel compelled to say that.'

Claudio spoke in Italian, the language his father had spoken to him. Matteo ignored it.

'New York closed with a ten percent decline in CC stock and London is just about to open. Tokyo will do so later. Your investors have abandoned you. You're done. By the end of the day you're not going to look so calm.'

Claudio merely shrugged. 'Again, your journey is wasted. The only pleasure is seeing you here. So much you remind me of Michele.'

'My father loved you, Claudio. My father loved you and look what you did to him.'

He hadn't known what he was going to say, had only known he needed to say something, but seeing the shock on Claudio's face he knew that he had hit the mark. Tears formed instantly in the man's eyes and his jaw clenched as he swallowed hard.

'He loved you. And my mother—and me. He was a good man who only wanted the best for all of us.'

'You didn't come here to tell me that. Why don't you say what you really want to say?'

'That I hate you? What good would that do? I've spent years doing that. Hating that you brought out a side of my dad that I never wanted to believe was true. But it was there, and maybe what you had together was beautiful once, but what you turned it into was sick and shameful, and you'll have to live with that for ever.'

'Michele was a coward...'

'He was my father,' Matteo said, launching himself across the room and grabbing Claudio by the collar in his two fists, bringing their faces inches apart. 'And my children will be brought up respecting his memory.'

Claudio was the coward. The fear was real in his eyes. Matteo shoved him away.

'Good luck in finding anyone who'll respect yours.'

CHAPTER SEVENTEEN

AT ELEVEN O'CLOCK precisely Ruby stepped from the bedroom and into the hallway. Light flooded down onto the mahogany floor…voices bubbled up from below. And panic clung to every fibre of her being.

'Go to the top of the stairs and then wait there,' whispered Coral behind her, resplendent in olive-green lace, scalloped-edged, knee-length and the perfect foil for her auburn hair.

Ruby looked at her fairy godmother-in-law, as she was beginning to think of her, and then, emboldened by her strong, unflinching presence, took the steps along to top of the stairway.

She looked at her feet in pointed cream satin shoes. Ahead a mirror showed her the image she still couldn't get used to. The dress—provided at short notice by the famous designer Giorgos, who just happened to be one of Matteo's closest friends—fitted her to perfection. Sleeveless, with a bodice cut sharply to reveal her collarbone, it dipped in a V that displayed a tiny hint of her cleavage. The empire line swelled into a tulip-shaped skirt, which ended mid-calf. Plain, simple, perfect. Her hair was piled high on her head, and a tiara of pearls held it in place.

The tiara was her 'old'—all the Rossini brides had worn it, and Coral had taken the greatest care in settling it onto her head. Her underwear was the 'blue'—silk and lace—and the 'borrowed' was the pearl and diamond earrings from Coral, which hung in simple perfection from her lobes.

The 'new' was the tissue-wrapped stockings she'd smoothed onto her legs and held in place with a suspender belt she'd never dreamed in a million years she'd wear. But the effect was lovely. And the thought of Matteo unfastening everything later was delicious.

She clutched a tied bouquet of orchid stems and stood there at the top of the stairs, waiting while Coral skirted past her. Then, as a trio of strings started to play one of her favourite pieces by Bach, they both started to walk down.

At the bottom, in a veil of sunbeams, she made her way through a pale-carpeted corridor to the room where Matteo stood, waiting. He wore a simple dark grey morning suit, a shirt as creamy as her dress, and no tie. But a little ivory rose poked above his breast pocket. His hair was swept back from his brow and brushed his collar. He turned and his brown berry eyes beamed right into hers and his mouth burst into a warm smile.

Her heart thudded in her chest and her knees

began to shake. The lump in her throat swelled and burned and tears threatened to spill from her eyes.

He saw her falter and a look swept his face. He turned round and with the full force of his body and the power of his stare drew her towards him, one step at a time.

My beautiful Ruby, he mouthed keeping his eyes trained on her. 'Absolutely beautiful,' he said aloud, when she took the final steps to him.

All she could do was nod as she took her place beside him for the wedding ceremony, barely aware of the rows of people behind and the indomitable Coral in her green dress by her side.

There were words and vows and rings, and despite no rehearsal he spoke clearly and confidently. And when he slid the solid gold band onto her finger she stared at it for a moment, almost unbelieving that it had actually happened.

Then he pulled her towards him and gazed down at her. And, oh, how she loved him—so much that she could burst. She loved his mind and his spirit. She loved his beautiful soul. She loved what he had done for her and she loved the thought of a future together with him. She could barely trust herself to hope her dream would come true. She loved him— loved every pore and nerve and fibre of his body. Only him.

He kissed her, and she told him with her lips how her heart beat only for him. And as he pulled back and smiled straight into her eyes, bathing her in warmth and tenderness, she knew he was finally going to say the words she had been longing to hear.

'Thank you,' he said. 'Thank you for making me the happiest man alive.'

Her heart flooded—but not with joy—and she fixed her smile into place. That was the moment. If he had felt love that was the moment he would have said it.

Coral rushed up to them, and then things swirled around her—from signing to smiling and posing for photographs. And the whole time she felt Matteo's arm around her shoulders or her waist, or his hand holding hers, whispers in her ear, stolen kisses.

'We'll get some pictures taken at the fountains later,' he said.

Her smile was still fixed. It was fine. This was how it was going to be. She loved him and he was happy.

'The happiest man alive.'

The most important thing was that her daughter was going to have a daddy. He was invested in their child. Coral too. She didn't need to worry.

But still that sickness spread through her—the terrifying fear that she would let them all down if she couldn't show love, be loved in return.

Matteo… What would happen when his deal went through? When he had his bank, his meetings and clients and charity benefits? When women would throw themselves at him?

He loved women. He loved sex.

He had married her, but only because he'd had to. He didn't *love* her. Not the way a husband really loved his wife.

And their daughter… What if she felt nothing for her child? What then?

She stood by his side on the terrace outside the room where they had just said their vows. In the distance the roofs of the Roman skyline spread out in a clutter of terracotta and gold all the way to the plains beyond. Flimsy white clouds trailed across the sky.

It was the perfect day to be married.

She couldn't wait for it to be over.

'Come on, Ruby, this is the happiest day of my life. You're my wife. We're going to have a baby. We're going to be happy. You're going to go back to your dancing. I can go back to sport—properly, maybe one day. We couldn't ask for more…'

He scooped her close to his body.

'Sweetheart, come on. Be happy.'

She pulled her smile as wide as it would go, made her eyes sparkle, squeezed out a tiny chuckle. 'I couldn't be any happier. I'm just as pleased as you are. Everything is going to be great, I know.'

Suddenly his face fell. His mouth hung open unhappily. His eyes bored into hers so fiercely that she had to bite her lip and look away. He shook his head and pulled her inside, along the hallway and into a room.

'I know you. You're faking this. You're unhappy

and you're making stuff up in your head. You're probably already planning how to get out of here.'

'No, I'm not,' she lied.

'Yes, you are.'

He stood there, this solid wall of man, and she knew that even if she closed her eyes she would still be able to feel him. His physical presence was like a power source for her now. She needed him so badly in order to keep going. Because if she was left on her own she would falter and fail. She couldn't leave now. She didn't have the strength any more.

'Promise me you won't go,' he said. 'Stay with me, Ruby, please. Don't take all this away. I need you.'

'I know you need me now. And I'd never abandon this after coming so far. But you won't need me for ever.'

'What are you saying?' he said, pulling her further into the room and closing the door. 'Of course I'm going to need you—our child will need both of us. Look at what we've got together. We have a brilliant relationship, we're totally compatible—we just got married, for God's sake. I know this felt like some crazy hare-brained scheme when we started, but it doesn't feel like that now, does it?'

'Come on, Matteo. If it wasn't for the baby we wouldn't be here.'

She turned away from his fierce gaze, stared past his shoulder at bookshelves full of ancient books piled high behind glass, at the dust mites that danced in the sunlight.

'Is that right?' he said softy. 'Come on. I want you to read this.'

He took her hand and walked her to the shelves. There he unlocked a glass cabinet. In it were rows of soft leather books, much slimmer than the rest. He pulled a black leather notebook from the end of the middle shelf.

'These are my journals. I've kept them since I was a kid. Occasionally I still write stuff down. This is the current one.'

He fanned the pages. Half of the book was filled with drawings and words; the other half was still empty. He looked at her and smiled. Held the book against his heart.

'You're in here,' he said.

They walked outside onto the terrace and down the steps towards the bubbling fountains. Shaded from the hot midsummer sun, they sat on a marble bench as the water sparkled in rainbows of spray all around them. He couldn't have chosen a more romantic spot, and her heart bubbled as much as the water around the stone nymphs.

'I've never let anyone read these. It's nobody's business. But this is about us, so it's yours too.'

She looked at it and recognised it as the book he'd been writing in on the boat.

He skimmed through it until he found the page he wanted. 'I wrote in this the day you told me you were pregnant. And the day after we met. And loads of other times too. Here—read.'

He opened it and handed it to her. She read what he had written in his decisive handwriting.

What a night!

Arturo is hopefully going to land in our lap, and I discovered a love of ballet.

OK, a love of a ballet dancer...

Met a woman and almost fell for her. Beautiful, sensitive, sensual. I'm pretty sure I'll call her. Once Arturo is in the bag...

First time I've felt like this in ages. Feel energised. Alive. Good times.

He took the book back, skimmed past more pages, then opened it again.

Can't get this woman out of my mind.

'So you can't pretend that this is all fake. This is the start of something wonderful.'

He looked at her with such kindness in his eyes, a kindness and warmth that she'd never seen from anyone before, and it felt like torchlight in the darkness—it felt as if she was being led in from the cold. Her heart thundered. It felt terrifying.

'You say that now, but you're hardly going to be here to be part of it. You're going to be away all the time, making deals and keeping people sweet, and pulling out the knives in your back that Claudio will be sticking in.'

He shook his head, all mirth wiped from his face like melting snow slipping into a river.

'We've still got a lot to talk about, but my days of being married to the job are over. I don't want to end up like my dad—though that wasn't just about the job. If Claudio hadn't been so in love with him none of this would have happened.'

She stared open-mouthed. 'What do you mean, in love with him?'

'Just what I say. They were lovers. I found out after the funeral, but out of respect for Mum I haven't said anything to anyone.'

Ruby stared up at the laughing stone cherubs, their innocent cheeks plump under the streaming fountains. Her head swam with all this news. So that was what this was all about. Claudio's jealousy had been driving him all these years. And Coral had never told anyone about it. How could she tell people that her husband had been gay? That brave, spirited woman must have suffered so much. And no one had known. She was a force of nature—an inspiration. And now she was her mother-in-law, too.

'Are you saying that's what drove your father to alcohol?'

'I'm saying that my dad was mixed up. He put his whole life into the bank and his family, but there was something deeply unhappy in him, and in the end it's what's killed him. Now Claudio has just announced that he's gay—that's why some of those old clients have left him.'

'And some people can't accept that? How ridiculous. Of all the underhand things Claudio's done, he's now being punished for being himself.'

'Yes, and, much as I want to build up the bank, I don't want to schmooze with people who hate like that. So I've decided.'

She heard the words. And the silence that followed. She turned. 'You've decided what?'

'I've decided that if Arturo wants to merge, that's fine. If he doesn't, that's also fine. Because I'm going to take the bank to market, make it public, and let someone else run it for a change. I'm not going to lose my life to it any more.'

She stared around the gardens. 'But what will you do? Are you going to go back to sport?'

He lifted her hand in his, wove their fingers together. The gold bands glinted in the sunlight.

'There are options—but that depends on you. We're going to have a baby. One of us is going to have to look after it while the other goes to work— that's how I see it. If you want to dance I'll stay home. If you want to stay home I'll go to work.'

The warm Italian afternoon was rolling on. Tall poplars swayed their ambivalence in the sunshine, this way or that way. Grass stood up in straight neat rows and the fountains bubbled contentedly. The Croydon park she'd once played in was a thousand miles from this. No gravelly play area, no graffiti walls, no mums pushing prams or sitting on benches, heads deep in their phones.

This life of sunshine was what her daughter should have—her grandmother and her father, sunshine and health. Happiness. Italy.

'You'll live here I take it...?' she said, her voice trailing off.

She couldn't speak any more, because the thought of what she would miss was choking her—her whole heart seemed to be tugging free and choking the very air from her body.

'I assumed you'd want to be based in England?' he said, turning her round.

She closed her eyes as she felt his warm, wonderful strength fold around her—her solid wall.

'Where do you want us to live? We don't need to decide right here, right now, but we're free to choose—we can be wherever we want. Ruby, we're free. *I* am free. For the past ten years I've been enslaved—as much as any of the slaves that fought in that Coliseum over there. Every day making myself do a job I didn't like, becoming a person I didn't want to be, showing disrespect to women.'

She looked up into his face and saw a brightness she'd never seen before. Hope shone from his eyes and his smile broadened widely. 'I'm so happy for you, Matteo. It must have been the hardest thing to decide, but it's the best news too.'

'I still don't think you get it, Ruby. This is the happiest day of my life. You have made me the happiest man alive. I don't care about anything else.'

He cupped her face, bent forward to kiss her, and

it felt different. It felt like the most possessive, passionate branding of his love.

'Do you love me?' she heard herself say.

'Do I love you? *Yes.* I've never met a woman like you. I've never seen such passion and spirit. You've set me an example that put me to shame, and when I asked you to, you stood by me. You were prepared to do anything for me and our little family. I won't ever forget that.'

She swallowed. 'You told me to pretend I loved you. I didn't need to pretend.'

'Me neither. We've got our lives ahead of us now. We'll work out where we want to be and what I'm going to do—maybe I'll coach. Who knows? But as long as we both know that we'll put our daughter first in all we do—that's all I ask. She needs to know she's the most important thing in the world to us.'

Ruby nodded. She knew more than anyone that her life's work was going to be making her daughter know that, in every fibre of her being. She knew that her only medicine was to fill up her soul with love, not fear.

'My father...' she said. 'I've never told you—or anyone, for that matter—but I've never met him. I only know his name and his home town. Will you help me find him? I really want to contact him now.'

He tucked her close and she buried herself against him, smelled him, breathed him in, and with every second felt replete with the power of his love.

'I'm so glad you've told me that. We'll find him

together. We'll work it all out together. And Coral is here for you as much as she is for me. For this one,' he said, stroking the soft curve of her stomach.

She smiled into his chest. Nodded. She finally knew.

She whispered the words she now understood.

'"Lovers don't finally meet someone. They're in each other all along."'

* * * *

If you enjoyed
The Tycoon's Shock Heir
why not explore these other stories
by Bella Frances?

The Argentinian's Virgin Conquest
The Italian's Vengeful Seduction
The Playboy of Argentina
The Consequence She Cannot Deny

Available now!

#3693 A DEAL FOR THE SICILIAN'S DIAMOND
Conveniently Wed!
by Michelle Smart
Aislin will do anything to secure money for her sick nephew—even pose as billionaire Dante's fiancée at a society wedding. Yet soon their explosive passion rips through the terms of their arrangement, leaving them both hungry for more...

#3694 THE PRINCE'S RUTHLESS WEDDING VOW
by Jane Porter
When Josephine rescues a drowning stranger, she's captivated. Until it's revealed that he's Prince Alexander, heir to the throne of Aargau... Now the threat of scandal means this shy Cinderella must become a royal bride!

#3695 INNOCENT QUEEN BY ROYAL COMMAND
Claimed by a King
by Kelly Hunter
King Augustus is shocked when his country delivers him a courtesan. But Sera's surprising innocence and undisguised yearning for him pushes Augustus's self-control to the limits. Now he won't rest until Sera becomes his queen!

#3696 BILLIONAIRE'S PRISONER IN PARADISE
by Annie West
Finding herself incognito and captive on Alexei's private island, Princess Mina must convince him *she's* his future bride. But after a night in the Greek's bed, there's more at stake than her hidden identity—her heart is at Alexei's mercy, too!

Get 4 FREE REWARDS!

We'll send you 2 FREE Books plus 2 FREE Mystery Gifts.

Harlequin Presents® books feature a sensational and sophisticated world of international romance where sinfully tempting heroes ignite passion.

FREE Value Over **$20**

HP19R

Aislin will do anything to secure money for her sick nephew—even pose as billionaire Dante's fiancée at a society wedding. Yet soon their explosive passion rips through the terms of their arrangement, leaving them both hungry for more…

Read on for a sneak preview of
Michelle Smart's next story,
The Sicilian's Bought Cinderella.

"But…" Aislin couldn't form anything more than that one syllable. Dante's offer had thrown her completely.

His smile was rueful. "My offer is simple, *dolcezza*. You come to the wedding with me and I give you a million euros."

He pronounced it *"seemple,"* a quirk she would have found endearing if her brain hadn't frozen into a stunned snowball.

"You want to pay me to come to a wedding with you?"

"Si." He unfolded his arms and spread his hands. "The money will be yours. You can give as much or as little of it to your sister."

It took a huge amount of effort to keep her voice steady. "But you must have a heap of women you could take and not have to pay them for it."

"None of them are suitable."

"What does that mean?"

"I need to make an impression on someone and having you on my arm will assist in that."

"A million dollars for one afternoon?"

"I never said it would be for an afternoon. The celebrations will take place over the coming weekend."

She tugged at her ponytail. "Weekend?"

"Aislin, the groom is one of Sicily's richest men. It is a necessity that his wedding be the biggest and flashiest it can be."

She almost laughed at the deadpan way he explained it.

She didn't need to ask who the richest man in Sicily was.

"If I'm going to accept your offer, what else do I need to know?"

"Nothing... Apart from that I will be introducing you as my fiancée."

"What?" Aislin winced at the squeakiness of her tone.

"I require you to play the role of my fiancée." His grin was wide with just a touch of ruefulness. The deadened, shocked look that had rung from his eyes only a few minutes before had gone. Now they sparkled with life, and it was almost hypnotizing.

She blinked the effect away.

"Why do you need a fiancée?"

"Because the father of the bride thinks going into business with me will damage his reputation."

"How?"

"I will go through the reasons once I have your agreement on the matter. I appreciate it is a lot to take in so I'm going to leave you to sleep on it. You can give me your answer in the morning. If you're in agreement then I shall take you home with me and give you more details. We will have a few days to get to know each other and work on putting on a convincing act."

"And if I say no?"

He shrugged. "If you say no, then no million euros."

Don't miss
The Sicilian's Bought Cinderella,
available February 2019 wherever
Harlequin Presents® books and ebooks are sold.

www.Harlequin.com

HPEXP0119R